StarLords

Talent For Trouble

BIANCA D'ARC

This book is a work of fiction. The names, characters, places, and incidents are products of the writer's imagination or have been used fictitiously and are not to be construed as real. Any resemblance to persons, living or dead, actual events, locale or organizations is entirely coincidental.

No part of this book may be used or reproduced in any manner whatsoever without written permission, except in the case of brief quotations embodied in critical articles and reviews.

DEDICATION

This book is dedicated to the fans who patiently waited for me to get back to this series.

It also marks the renewal of an editing relationship that started way back in 2005 with my first book, *Maiden Flight*. For that reason, I'd like to thank Jess Bimberg, my first—and current—editor. We've come full circle, and the band is back together! Woohoo!

And last, but certainly not least, to my Dad (who will never read this book!), for hanging tough through major heart surgery earlier this year and sticking around to continue to dispense his wisdom and words of encouragement. I love you, Dad.

.

CHAPTER ONE

Jana Olafsdotter, native of Mithrak, was kept under heavy guard in the main medical facility on Geneth Mar. Her highly ranked sister, Jeri, was allowed to visit, and did so regularly, but Jana was still under a healer's care, and probably would be for a very long time to come.

She didn't remember much about her life since being taken from the family farm somewhere around her sixteenth birthday. At odd times, she heard malevolent chanting in the recesses of her mind where nothing of the kind ought to be. That, and the sparkling blue crystals that had fused to her skin during a horrific explosion of psi power, was the only proof of what they claimed she had been doing this past decade or more.

Really, she had no way of knowing how long she had been under the collective's control. She also had no way of knowing what she had done with her strong Talent under their command. She only knew what she'd been told, along with hazy, and sometimes alarmingly clear, snippets of memories. She had been horrified by where she was and what she'd been doing in those few memories—and what had been done to her.

She knew enough to fear the person she had been and the things she had done. In the dark of night, ghosts of memories haunted her, and she woke screaming more often than not.

She had been a leader of the assault fleet and had attacked her own sister in the skies above Liata. She knew all about Liata now, of course. She had learned it was a peaceful, mainly agricultural world that had few defenses and little to steal. But the Wizards' collective and their allies wanted it under their control, and they had sent her out with a fleet of ships to get it by any means necessary.

She had rained destruction on the pastoral planet, and ruined many lives in the process. Even now, her misdeeds haunted her, though if she had been in control of her mind, she never would have used her powers for such evil work. She preferred peace, when it could be had. And, though she would fight to defend others, the Jana she had once been, and wanted again to be, would never harm another without provocation.

Except maybe that frustratingly annoying man.

Darak, they called him. They all bowed and scraped to him, calling him *master* and *lord*. It was enough to make her howl.

He was so condescendingly masculine. He flirted shamelessly with every female in the facility. It didn't matter if they were eight or eighty. He flirted with them all.

And they all acted like silly girls when he smiled at them. From the oldest to the youngest, they indulged him and sent simpering smiles his way. They also took the trouble to remind Jana almost daily about how she owed her life to him and how she should be nicer to him.

But it was impossible to be nice to him. Every time she saw him, she wanted to pounce on him. And not in a good way.

He had crafty eyes that held far too much knowledge. His smug expression led her to think scandalous things about this man and her little sister—and her little sister's new husband. Could it be?

It was unthinkable.

She knew things were different on Council worlds, but

she'd been raised on Mithrak, where people simply didn't behave in the manner she'd witnessed during her short stay on this planet. On Mithrak, sex was had in pairs—if it was had at all—and only under the blessing of the collective and their representatives. Among Wizards, or Talents as they called them here, sex was tightly controlled and meant for procreation alone, unless otherwise sanctioned by higher authority within the collective.

The collective had tried to breed her several times. The seed had never taken, and she was glad. They had punished her for defiance, but she hadn't liked the brutal invasion of her body by the horrid men they'd chosen. Every one of them had been much older than she, and more psychically powerful. She remembered each encounter in intimate detail, for the men had shielded her mind from the collective and suborned her consciousness to themselves instead for their bestial attacks.

She almost wished she didn't remember what they'd done to her and made her do in return. It made her feel dirty inside and out, and she didn't think she could ever join with another man again, for any reason. She certainly didn't see why the women of the Council worlds put up with it. And, sometimes, with multiple partners, no less.

There had to be something about sex that she was missing, but she definitely did not want to take the chance of further pain and humiliation to find out. She was better off celibate. Considering she was basically living in a med facility, that didn't present much of a problem.

Only when that bastard Darak came and smiled so knowingly at her, did she have pangs of regret, or something almost like regret. She didn't quite know what she felt when he came to her and checked on her progress, extending his healing power so gently and caressing her little hurts—the tender scars where the blue crystals had fused with her skin.

No one else bothered with those, but he did. It made her feel funny inside, though she didn't have a name for what she was feeling. It was something she had never experienced before.

* * *

Jana was dozing lightly in her hospital bed when she felt a light touch on her cheek and then the tingling sensation she knew so well by now. Sure enough, when she opened her eyes, there stood Darak the Dreadful in all his magnificent, roguish glory.

"Did you miss me, doll?"

She would have answered rudely, but he chose that moment to zap her with his incredible healing touch that always made her feel good.

"Why do you do that? No one else bothers with the scars. They're just happy to have me breathing." She moved away, annoyed with him just for being so devastatingly handsome. She didn't want to be attracted to any man, much less him.

Darak's rich chuckle sounded through the room and bathed her senses in warmth. She would have shivered if she'd allowed herself to show even that much pleasure in his presence.

"Think of it as my way of apologizing for not being able to get those shards out of your skin." He caressed her shoulder, the place where her neck met her collarbone, where just one of the bright blue jewels had taken up residence. When the stone at the center of her scepter had exploded in that last battle, shards of the power-infused crystal had embedded themselves in her skin, and nobody had yet found a way to get them out. "They do look rather pretty, though, you have to admit. I bet your whole body sparkles."

"They're a constant reminder of a past I'd rather forget."

Darak frowned, and it was the first time she had ever seen such a dark look on his handsome face. It made him seem almost human.

"You should be reminded instead of your bravery and strength, and the hard path you've taken to get here. Your mind is free now, Jana. You'll never be under their control again."

"How can you be sure of that?" Her whispered words revealed just how afraid she was that somehow the collective would reclaim her and her power.

Darak scooped her easily into his arms, holding her close. She allowed it, feeling safe and secure in his strong embrace in a way she hadn't since she'd grown too old for her father's bear hugs. Darak—as annoying as he was—always made her feel safe. Because of that, she let him take liberties that would have her screaming for help should anyone else attempt them.

"I'm sure because you're a strong woman, Jana. And you have powerful friends. Your sister is a Sha, married to another Sha, for goodness sake. They alone can hold off the entire Wizard collective, and you don't think for one moment they'd ever let you be hurt again, do you? Plus, since your sister married my cousin, we're family of a sort. I would help you if you needed it, but Jana, sweetheart..." His gaze held hers with grave seriousness. "I don't think you'll need it. You're strong enough to stand on your own against whatever comes your way. I can read that truth in your beautiful eyes."

"But the stones..." She whispered her greatest fear. "The stones in my skin will always connect me to the collective. Even now, I can hear them murmuring in the back of my mind."

Darak hugged her tight, placing a kiss on the crown of her head. A single sparkling shard of stone had lodged just below and to the right of her right eye, highlighting the blueness of her eyes, the clarity of her gaze. The scepter of power had been in her right hand when it blew up, and he knew from treating her wounds in those first hours that most of the splinters of that huge jewel had embedded themselves in odd patterns all along her right side, though a few other memorable ones spanned her petite frame.

"They will never control you again. I promise."

"How can you say that?"

He pulled back and stared deep into her eyes. "Because I

believe in you, Jana." He leaned in and kissed her lips sweetly, briefly, shockingly, before pulling back once more. "When I healed you, I went deeper than I ever have before. I touched your soul, little one. And what I saw there was so breathtakingly beautiful, I know deep in my heart that you're free. Your bright spirit will never allow itself to be taken over again."

A tear streaked down the side of her face, past the glinting reminders of what she had been through. He leaned in and licked it away as her breath caught in her throat.

"What if I'm not strong enough?" All her fear was in her stark words, condensed and trembling.

"You are. But, as I keep reminding you, you're not in this alone, anymore. You have your sister and new brother-in-law behind you. Not to mention me. Though my power is nowhere near Jeri's or Micah's, I'm still considered one of the more Talented folks here. I can help you as I have before. I won't let anyone undo the work I've put into saving your life. I promise you that."

He lifted her chin with tender fingers and kissed her again, this time lingering a bit longer, licking her lips as if seeking entrance. Something fluttered low in her belly, but she didn't recognize the sensation. It felt good, but it was frightening, too.

She opened her mouth to tell him to leave her alone, but she never got the chance as his tongue swept inside. He stroked her mouth gently, tangling his tongue with hers and enticing her to come out and play.

She found herself responding before she really even knew what she was doing, and the tingling in her tummy turned to hot, molten fire. She clamped her legs together as she felt the unaccustomed heat. Something strange was happening, and it had to stop. She was afraid.

When Darak's hand moved down to toy with her breast, she found the strength to push him away in her momentary panic. She held him by the wrist, but his gaze was kind, his expression soft in a way she never would have expected.

"Don't do that again, Darak. I mean it."

He turned his wrist and, somehow, came up with her hand gently cradled in his long, strong fingers. He brought it to his lips and kissed her gallantly.

"That, I cannot promise, sweetheart. I like kissing you. And, judging by your reaction, you like kissing me, too."

Her senses screamed at her to let him continue, but her mind was saying stop. She knew to which she should listen.

"If you try it again, I'll bite you."

His chuckle was wicked. "You promise?"

The silly, leering grin on his face almost made her want to laugh, but she reminded herself just in time how dangerous this man was. She didn't want to fall under his spell as so many other women did on a daily basis. He had the entire female staff of this facility making eyes at him, and even some of the men sent admiring glances his way. Some wanted him, but most wanted to *be* him. It was disgusting. Really.

"You're looking stronger every day, Jana."

She was relieved when he changed the subject and let her go. She lay back on the bed as he moved to the window, lifting the gauzy curtain to peer out at the green grounds.

"They have me doing therapy, and I can sit up and even walk for longer and longer each time."

"So your doctors tell me. Which brings me to another thing." He turned to face her, and she had a momentary pang of fear from the serious look on his handsome face. "When you're better, the Council would like to question you."

"I expected as much. I don't remember a lot, but I will freely give what information I can."

"I told them that would be your answer, but you will face some skeptics. Be prepared for a little hostility. Some of them see you as an enemy, and it will take time to make them understand just how fully you were under the collective's control." His gaze hardened. "But they need to know, Jana. For that reason alone, it's important that you submit to their questions. They don't understand our enemy, and that could be a fatal mistake. They need to know how the collective operates and why you and those few ship captains took the chance to defect when Jeri and Micah shattered your control crystal."

Just the mention of the huge blue gem that was now splintered and embedded in her skin made her shiver. Darak saw the fear coursing through her and stepped forward, but he didn't dare take her in his arms again. That way lay madness. He couldn't hold her without wanting to have her in every way a man could have a woman. He wanted her in his bed, in his home, in his life. And that thought was truly scary.

"Jana, I've been thinking long and hard about those jewels you wear so prettily." His voice was deliberately coaxing. "The Wizards used the larger stone to control you and the other ship captains. But what if you learned how to use the crystal shards in your skin to focus your own Talent against the collective?"

He sensed she was considering his words. He'd gotten her attention. Now, he just had to get her mind working on the problem.

"Do you think it can be done?" he asked, drawing her gaze.

"I don't know. But it's an interesting thought."

"Those who live on Council worlds don't use stones to focus our Talent. In fact, we've never seen anything like the shards the Council has been analyzing. The ones I was able to get out of your skin. Do you know where the crystal is from?"

"I have no idea. But I do remember that we feared the blue stones and the Wizards that wielded them, even as children. They are the mark of a high-level Wizard, and they were the ones that would come and take children away from their parents."

"If I'm right and the crystal connected you to the collective while you were so far out of their home range, then it's possible that targeting the crystals of other Wizards will also put them out of commission."

"Except for the fact that the psi wave released when Jeri and Micah shattered my crystal almost killed me and would have burned every Talent within a parsec of the blast had Jeri and Micah not been there. Only their shielding allowed everyone to live through that unharmed."

"Unharmed, perhaps." An ironic smile lifted the corner of his sensual mouth. "But not unchanged."

"That's when you rose from Dominar to Master Mage, right? You skipped right over one of your Council's highest rankings, as did the other people on your ship, Jeri told me."

"And we haven't completely figured out what it did to you, yet. Aside from your new, all-too-permanent jewelry, that is."

"I've been too wrung out emotionally, physically and psychically, to even attempt to use my Talent. I don't even know if it's still there."

"Oh, it's there all right." Darak grinned at her. "I can feel it snapping along my nerve endings. It's there, and it's strong. Never fear."

"But, without direction of the collective, I'm basically untrained. The healers here have warned me not to try focusing on anything until I'm fully healed and they can arrange a base-level test and some strong shielding."

"I think Jeri wants to be with you when that starts. Micah, as well. Their honeymoon is nearly over, so they can be with you when you're ready to try again."

Darak noticed the way Jana stiffened at the mention of her sister, but didn't understand the reason for her reaction. He knew she loved her sister, and vice versa, but was there some problem between the siblings? If so, they'd have to work it out. They needed each other, as far as he was concerned. Family was important. Too important to allow a misunderstanding to linger and corrupt the relationship.

"You think I need two Shas to shield me? Are you that worried about what the stone might have done to me?"

"Yes." Darak watched her carefully as he leveled with her.

"I know for a fact that Jeri is worried, too, and wants to be with you."

"Just how well do you *know* my little sister?"

The question took him totally off guard. He reared back a bit in surprise.

"What kind of question is that?"

"You heard me. You speak of her as if… as if…"

"As if I've been inside her?" He deliberately pitched his voice low, watching the furious flush rise in her cheeks. Her raw Talent sparked along his senses, and it made him hot in more ways than one.

"You're disgusting." She turned her face away from him.

"No." He spoke softly as he sat on the side of her bed. "Just truthful." He sighed heavily. "I have loved your sister."

She didn't think her heart could take the pain that lanced through it at his admission.

"Love? You call that love?" She couldn't fathom this culture or the way they shared their bodies so freely. She just did not understand it.

"A small part of my heart will always be hers, just as a small part of her thinks of me fondly. But she loves my cousin deeply and truly, in a way that I've never experienced. They belong together. Micah will care for her all the days of their lives."

"Then, why in the world would he let you…?" The question slipped out before she could censor her words.

"Fuck her?"

She gasped at the blunt word, and Darak sighed heavily. He moved closer on the soft mattress, but didn't touch her.

"I know you and Jeri were raised on Mithrak and that your culture is different from ours." He shook his head, as if frustrated. "Our people discovered, not long after the Council was formed, that those with Talent have a way of reenergizing each other through sexual pleasure. Though first joinings can be dangerous, once the energies are aligned, the giving and receiving of pleasure can enhance our natural

Talents, recharge us and heal those in need of psi energy." He looked back at her, pinning her with his dark gaze. "This was discovered several centuries ago by the Founders of our Council, you understand. Over the years since then, joinings among Talents became more open, more free. Micah and I, as well as just about everyone who lives on a Council world, were raised to give and receive pleasure freely."

"So, you're telling me that my little sister sleeps with anyone she pleases? I thought she was married!" Her anger was getting the better of her, but there was no way not to get angry at the thought of her innocent little sister being victimized by these Council brutes.

"That's not what I'm telling you at all." Darak's voice was calm. How could he be so blasted calm when he was talking about having sex with her sister? "Jeri was on the run for most of her life. I don't know all the details, but she did tell me that after the Wizards took you and murdered your parents, they hunted her. She hid among the horses, eventually stowing away aboard a ship bound for Pantur. Even there, she wasn't free. The Hill Tribes share pleasure almost as openly as we do, but she never joined in. She came to my cousin a virgin."

"She told you that?" She couldn't imagine her little sister speaking so frankly about such private things.

Darak grinned wickedly. "No. He did."

Just like a man to discuss his conquests with his buddy. She was disgusted. But then why did she feel just a tiny flicker of flame low in her belly? It must be anger, she decided. All men were swine.

"I'm not getting a very good impression of my new brother-in-law." Her voice was purposely haughty, but it didn't appear to affect Darak in the least. He winked at her, and she sniffed and turned her head.

"My point is that Micah wanted to give her the experiences we all grew up taking for granted. We've shared pleasure in many different and varied ways. I've seen and done enough to know that when I saw Micah and Jeri together, I was witnessing something almost sacred." Now, Darak looked away from her as if he didn't want her to see too closely. "Micah knew he loved Jeri, almost from the moment he found her. But he was afraid, I think, that because she'd never been with anyone but him, she didn't really know her own heart. He let her fly free. He gave her the experiences that all young women on our worlds usually have and stood by her, sharing in her pleasure, showing by example that his love made every moment they had together more special than a mere joining of bodies and sharing of pleasure. What they share is love in its purest form."

Silence reigned a long, long moment. She didn't think he'd meant to say so much. He refused to look at her, apparently lost in thought, but she could feel discomfort coming off him in waves. She was empathic enough, even without focusing her Talent, to know that he was uncomfortable with the revelations he'd just made. She let the moment pass, saying nothing.

"It was my honor to join with Jeri and Micah, and normally, I wouldn't entertain questions about my activities, but you have a right to know." His eyes met hers steadily. "I want the air clear between us. I joined with your sister, but I doubt I will ever be invited to do so again."

Her eyes narrowed. He was trying to convey something to her, but she didn't quite understand what lay beneath his words.

"Would you? If you were asked now?"

Slowly, he shook his head.

"No. Not now." His hand covered hers, resting atop her upper thigh. "Not ever again."

Could he mean...? No. No way. Even she could see this man was a playboy. He went from woman to woman like bees went from flower to flower. So, maybe he wouldn't sleep with Jeri again, but there was no way he'd give up his wanton ways. Every other woman was fair game. Including, it seemed, she herself.

His hand stroked her fingers, warming her from the inside

out. It made her uncomfortable, but she could hardly object. He wasn't overstepping the bounds of propriety. Yet.

But she knew he would. It was in his nature. This man liked to push the envelope in all ways, and she feared he would push her as far as she'd go. It was up to her to push back.

Her experiences with men were nothing but bad, traumatic memories. She wouldn't be tempted to let this rogue into her pants anytime soon.

She hoped.

But he had a way about him…

"You're thinking too hard, Jana." Darak tapped her temple lightly then wrapped his palm around the nape of her neck in a gesture of comfort. "Give it time."

There was so much more he wanted to say to her. Things that had been rattling around in his brain since almost the first moment he'd touched her. She'd been so badly injured and near death after that last battle. Uncomfortable things surfaced in his mind that had him questioning his own sanity, his feelings, his future.

He was starting to think that she *was* his future. And that scared him spitless. But he tried to follow the same advice he'd just given her. He was letting things happen and leaving a lot up to fate. He didn't know where these startling new feelings were coming from, and he didn't know where they'd lead, but he wanted to find out. No, he *needed* to find out.

He had to feel her body against his again, just for a moment. Darak pulled her as gently as he could into his arms. She didn't protest; though, at first, she was a bit stiff as he rubbed comforting circles on her back.

"Just relax, Jana. Let it all go. Tomorrow will take care of itself." He nestled his head next to hers, breathing in the fresh spring fragrance of her hair. She made him feel good in a way he hadn't felt in a long time. "Your only job now is to finish healing. Then, I'll take you to the Council."

She tensed at his words. "I'm not looking forward to

that."

He stroked her softly, sending out a tendril of his healing energy into the scars that caused her small hurts, wishing he could heal her mind as easily.

"I'll be with you every step of the way, Jana."

She pulled back, her face scrunched up in confusion as she watched him.

"Why, Darak? Why are you being so kind to me?"

"Because I have to. I don't know why, but I know you need me, and I need to be there for you."

"This is more than a healer looking after his patient, isn't it?" She sounded suspicious.

"Yes, that's true. Though, in some remote areas of this galaxy, people still believe that if you save a life, you are responsible for that person for the rest of their lives."

"You have no responsibility toward me."

"Ah, but there you're wrong. Not only because you're now a cousin-in-law. There's more to it than that. Some connection formed when I healed you, I guess. It's more…" He found it hard to describe what he felt. "It's something I can't explain."

She shocked him by placing her warm little palm against his heart, pressing close.

"I was empathic, even as a child, Darak. Even without focusing my Talent, I can feel a little of what you're feeling." She closed her eyes, concentrating without drawing on her Talent. That would have been too dangerous. But the energy currents lived in the air around all beings, they both knew, and that might be enough for her to learn entirely too much about what drove him now.

He pulled back, and her eyes opened in confusion.

"Don't do it, Jana. You don't want to know what I'm feeling."

She tilted her head to the side, studying him.

"Why not?"

"Because you're not ready for it." His voice dropped low, and his gaze held hers as the tension between them grew thick.

"Not ready for what? The truth?"

"The truth…" he tugged her a little roughly back into his arms, "…and this." His lips met hers with a passion he hadn't yet shown her. He devoured her mouth, licking, sucking and even nipping his way past all her defenses. She moaned as he started a rhythm with his tongue that was echoed in her suddenly aching pussy.

CHAPTER TWO

Darak came to visit her again, several weeks later. It was the longest he'd gone between visits, and Jana was sure his neglect had to do with the rather strong emotions he had revealed during his last visit. She didn't bring it up and neither did he, each very circumspect in their conversation while Healer Barath checked her a final time.

Barath was a Specitar who excelled only in healing, and that to a very great degree. He had overseen her treatment, and he took a moment to explain what had been done with her injuries to Darak, though he had never done so before to her knowledge. Yet, Darak seemed to know too much about her specific injuries as she listened to him talk with the older man—more than he should have known from just his initial treatment of her to save her life.

She eyed him suspiciously until the old healer left the room.

"What?" The smirk was back, and it served as a warning to her. Darak was in his typical devilish mood.

"You've been checking up on me."

He nodded, not embarrassed in the least to be caught. "The Council asked me to keep tabs on your progress since I have some healing ability and was already familiar with your injuries."

She sat back against her pillows, deflated for a moment, but she still didn't trust him.

"I don't understand how your rankings work. Why are you a Master Mage and Barath a Specitar? What makes you any different from him and vice versa?"

Darak sat in the visitor chair, sprawling negligently. If he'd calculated his posture, it couldn't be sexier, she thought. But it just came to this rogue naturally.

"Ah, I think I understand. Specitars only have one or, at most, two psi abilities. Their Talent is very directed, totally channeled to their specific abilities, and they excel in those areas. But only in those areas. It's a relatively rare condition. Most of us have Talent in a broader range of things. For example, I can heal, but I also have telepathic and some telekinetic abilities. I can channel my power to any number of tasks, not just healing or 'pathing or whatever. Barath can only heal. That's it. He's a one-trick pony. But that one trick, he does better than anyone else."

"So, how do they rank Specitars? How do they know who's the strongest among them?"

"There are relatively few of them. In order to become a Specitar, you have to manifest your one Talent at Mage level or above. From what I've seen, Specitars tend to group themselves by what they do. The telepaths gravitate toward each other, the healers to healers, and so on. Among themselves, they get to know who has the strongest ability, and they sort themselves out, I think. They have their own Council that is part of the larger Mage Council, and they handle specific tasks unique to their abilities—teaching, testing and the like."

"It sounds very complicated." Jana scratched her head as she thought through what he'd just told her. "The collective was so different. We were all just cogs in the wheel, and the Voice told us who would lead and what to do at all times."

"The Voice?" Darak seemed suddenly interested and alert, though his slouching posture hadn't changed.

"The Voice of the collective. At least, that's what I call it.

It was what, or perhaps *who*, gave all the orders. I can still hear it murmuring in the back of my mind, but I think it's unaware of me."

This time, he sat up. "How do you know?"

"If it knew I was within hearing, it would give me orders. It would try to control me again." She looked at him as if he were slow. Fear shot through her at the thought, making her shiver. "It doesn't know I can still hear it. If it ever finds out, I'm done for."

Darak sat on the edge of her bed, reaching out one hand to stroke her hair. "I seriously doubt that, Jana."

"Why?"

"Besides two very angry Shas and one Mage Master standing firmly between you and the collective, there's your own very strong Talent. I doubt you would ever succumb to their dominion again. Not now that you're fully aware of it." He stood, letting her go. "Come, we have places to go and things to do today. I've come to officially spring you from this facility and escort you to the family. Jeri and Micah arrived back yesterday and your sister wants very much to see you."

They went in a small private craft that Darak piloted expertly. The family compound was huge, richly appointed, and beautiful. The wealth and power of this family was not lost on Jana. She noted the graceful architecture and sprawling lands. She saw horses, too, roaming freely in one huge area that had been set aside for them, probably at her sister's request. Darak had told Jana about Micah's wedding gift to his bride—a tropical island where her horses could roam free.

Jana hadn't realized until that moment how she had missed the herds of huge beasts that she'd been raised to train. Most of her childhood teaching was forgotten or suppressed by the collective's training, but she felt a yearning to be as free as those majestic animals she saw galloping below the small craft as they came in for a landing.

"Jeri has had quite an effect on our family lands already.

The herd came when she called, and now, they won't leave." Darak apparently saw the direction of her gaze.

She could feel his admiration for the beasts, though, belying his gruff words. "Do you know horses? Do you ride?"

"Not well. Though it is something I've always wanted to learn."

She was amazed that he'd give such information to her so freely. This was not a man used to exposing any sort of weakness, and she doubted he failed at any endeavor he tried, but then, perhaps he had another motive in revealing so much. Perhaps he was making a sort of peace offering, letting her feel superior in some small way while she was so completely within his control.

"Maybe I can teach you a thing or two about riding. That is, if I remember how myself." She chuckled as the horses left her line of sight and the craft descended. "It's been too long."

He landed the craft skillfully, reinforcing her impression of his capabilities. Darak seemed to excel at just about anything he tried. No doubt he would prove an able rider, as well, for all his protestations. But riding would have to wait. She was still pretty weak and unable to get very far on her own. Darak, in fact, had to help her stand and support her on one side.

He hit the control that would open the ship and lower the ramp, and then, he walked her out, helping her with each careful step down the incline. She was watching her feet intently, hoping to avoid a fall. She didn't see the undignified ball of energy that was her sister come hurtling up the steep ramp to engulf her in a hug until it was nearly too late to avoid a spill.

But Darak was there, supporting them both, his strong arms surrounding Jana from behind while Jeri gripped her from the front.

"Jana!" Jeri's voice came to her through tears and tight squeezes. Jana was not altogether surprised to feel an answering wetness on her own cheeks.

"Little Jeri-berry. Thank the stars." Jana couldn't say more then, completely overcome by emotion as she hugged Jeri close.

She felt Darak leave her, secure enough on her feet now with Jeri's tight embrace. She missed his warm presence, but she needed this time with her little sister. Goddess, how she'd missed her!

They hugged and cried, each overwhelmed by the other's presence. It was a low male voice that finally broke through their joyful tears. A voice Jana did not recognize.

"You two should probably come inside where we can sit. There is much to discuss." The voice was gentle, concerned, and she could tell it wasn't just concern for Jeri, but for Jana as well. She knew her legs were trembling, and the man, whoever he was, could probably see it plainly. Suddenly, she realized who the tall man must be.

"You're Micah?"

Jeri pulled back and reached out one hand to the man, bringing him closer. There were stars in her eyes when she looked at him. Jana almost envied the love she read in her sister's gaze; for it was obvious these two were very much in love with each other, even to her.

"Jana, this is my husband."

"Darak has told me much about you, Lord Micah."

"All of it bad, I'm sure." He winked at her, his smile disarming as he led them indoors. Instantly, Darak was at her side, his strong arm ready to support her as she took slow steps toward the nearby doorway.

"I only spoke the truth, Micah. Can I help it if you're a troublemaker?" Darak joked easily with his cousin, a twinkle in his eye that was enchanting.

Jeri laughed. "I think you have that the other way around, Dar. Micah's a saint compared to you."

"Now that, I believe." Jana spoke before she even realized she would, surprising herself as they all laughed. Darak's arm squeezed her as he helped her inside, but she could tell he was enjoying her joke, not upset at all by her words.

They sat together for over an hour, sipping cool drinks

brought by quiet and efficient servants, catching up on all that had happened. At times, Jeri and Jana were nearly overwhelmed by emotion, but Micah would pull Jeri into his arms and she would find comfort there, much as Darak's strong presence at her side did for Jana. She realized something else after a time—her sister was shielding her, holding her safe within incredibly powerful shields that didn't allow anything in to possibly hurt her while, at the same time, protecting her from her own unpredictable energies.

She had never heard of anything like it before, but then, she had never met anyone with her sister's level of power before. It was truly amazing.

Jana grew silent as the full reality of what was happening hit her.

"What is it?" Darak, as usual, was the first to note the change in her.

Jana blinked at her baby sister. "Jeri, I didn't truly appreciate before how strong you've grown." Her words were hesitant as she sent out the barest of probes to test the phenomenon that was surrounding her, keeping her safe even from herself.

"Don't, Jana." Micah's voice was firm as he reached forward to take her hand. "Until you've had time to heal more, you shouldn't try to harness even the smallest of your abilities. It could do further damage."

Jana stopped at once, her eyes wide with horror. "Oh, no! Did I hurt you?"

Jeri laughed, but not unkindly. "Micah meant you could damage yourself further. We've been holding the pain away, but without it, you might not realize if you pushed a little too far."

"Holding the pain away? You can do that?" Jana gasped.

"We thought it was best during this first meeting," Micah answered. "I know strong emotion can bring out unexpected spikes in Talent, and we didn't want you hurt by this meeting, so we've been cushioning you, if you will."

"Wow."

"I told you your little sis had done well," Darak teased. "She and my cousin are two of the most powerful beings in the galaxy, but I help make sure it doesn't go to their heads."

Jeri threw a soft pillow at him, which he pretended hurt. He was rubbing his "injury" so dramatically Jana couldn't help but chuckle. She realized in that moment that Darak was very good at disarming almost any situation with humor.

The men finally left the two sisters alone for a short time, using the excuse that they wanted to go over specs for the refit of the *Circe*. Jeri knew full well Darak had everything in hand with the ship that used to be her husband's command, but appreciated the fact that they had made some effort to make their leaving seem uncontrived.

She wanted time alone to get to know her older sister again. They had been apart for so long, subjected to horrors neither one fully knew about the other. They had much to talk about and much to learn if they were to regain the loving relationship they had once shared.

"I missed you so much, Jana."

"I remember the Wizards taking me and how you hid. I knew they hadn't gotten you, though I saw them... I saw them kill Mother and Dad." Her voice grew soft with painful memory. "They wanted me to see it. It was part of their conditioning. They wanted me to know I had no home to return to."

"The devils!" Jeri was incensed by the pain she saw in her sister's eyes.

"They are that," Jana agreed with a wry twist of her lips. "Perhaps it's a blessing in disguise that I don't remember very much of my time under their control."

"You don't?"

Jana shook her head, her eyes trained on something only she could see. "It's foggy. I sometimes see moments of clarity, but they're out of context for the most part. Only a few times was I completely free of the collective, for mating purposes, and those times, I'd rather not remember at all."

"Mating purposes?" Jeri didn't think she liked the sound of that.

Jana nodded absently. "They try to breed more Wizards by choosing the more powerful females to breed to the ruling males. More than a few times, when they'd determined I was fertile, they shut me out from the collective and put me in a room. A male would arrive shortly thereafter and have sex with me. Thankfully, a child never resulted, and after a while, they took me out of the rotation and put me back on the front lines. I was more use to them there."

"Jana, I don't know what to say. I take it the sex wasn't exactly consensual." Jeri kept her voice low and cautious.

Jana laughed, but it wasn't a pleasant sound. "Are you kidding? I felt filthy when they were done with me. I welcomed the collective then, when I never had before. With them all in my mind, directing me, I didn't have to remember..." She sobbed then, but quickly brought herself under control.

Jeri moved close to her older sister, putting her arms around her tentatively. It was amazing to think that she knew more about the good side of sex than her older sister did. It was obvious Jana was traumatized by what had been done to her and it wasn't something she would get over easily.

"Jana, I was virgin until I met Micah, and I've loved every moment of being with him. That's the way it's supposed to be between male and female."

Jana pulled back from her, accusation in her eyes. "Even when your so-called husband was sharing you with Darak?"

Jeri was shocked speechless for a moment. "Darak told you about that?"

"I guessed. He merely confirmed it."

Jeri sat back. "I see. Then, you should know this. I love my husband with all my heart. It was his gift to me to give me the experiences the women here grow up taking for granted. I enjoyed it. Every moment of it. But that doesn't mean it's something I need. I need only Micah, and he needs only me."

"Are you sure about that?"

"Absolutely." Jeri responded in a firm voice. "We are joined in heart and in mind. I know his desires as he knows mine."

"You desire Darak still?"

Jeri finally understood. It was jealousy that drove her sister. Jealousy, fear and a tiny spark of curiosity? This would bear watching. Jeri couldn't think of a better mate for her older sister than Darak. She knew intimately that under his playboy exterior lived the heart of a true hero.

"No. I never desired Darak, or any man, as I do Micah."

"You wound me." Darak's playful voice came from the doorway, alerting the women to the men's return. "And here I thought you would pine for me for the rest of your days."

Jeri laughed up at him as he swooped down to place a smacking kiss on her lips.

"Unhand my wife, Dar, or face the consequences."

Micah's words were threatening, but his eyes glinted with laughter as he bounced down onto the couch next to Jeri, pulling her close to his side. Darak simply plucked Jana up in his strong arms and carried her to the adjoining chair where he sat with her in his lap. She tried to fight free for a brief moment, but he stilled her with a soft kiss to her temple and a brushing caress of his hands down her arms.

"So, are we talking about sex?" Darak's sense of humor sparkled in his eyes. "I hope we didn't miss anything good."

"As far as I'm concerned, the words good and sex don't belong in the same sentence."

Jana's bald words silenced all in the room momentarily, but it was Darak that eased the tension. He squeezed her tight in comfort.

"You will never have reason to fear intimacy among our people, Jana. I vow it."

"But you will consult a mind healer first thing tomorrow. I'll have Master Toombs flown in to see you." Micah's soft tone brooked no argument. "Such hurts must be attended. Sexual abuse is rare among the Council worlds, but sadly, it does happen from time to time, and we have professionals who can help you deal with it."

Jana fought her way out of Darak's lap to stand shakily by the window, effectively shutting out everyone else in the room. It was Darak who moved up behind her, there for her if she should fall on her wobbly legs.

"My cousin is right, Jana. You need to talk to someone about this. It's not good for you to be so traumatized by your past."

His voice was as soft and caring as Jeri had ever heard it, and she felt more than saw her sister's response to him. Perhaps there was something already between the two. In truth, nothing would make Jeri happier, but she knew both of them had a long way to go before either could share their lives with another.

Darak had a great deal to prove to himself, if to no one else, so he could climb out from behind Micah's shadow. Jana had the obvious trauma of the collective to deal with and put behind her so she could try to start anew, living here on a Council world. Jeri was troubled by thoughts of their rocky future, but the idea that they could find peace and happiness together, as she had found with Micah, gave her hope.

She saw Micah making a few notes on the nearby comm unit, summoning the gifted mind healer, Master Toombs, to their residence tomorrow, and she squeezed his hand in thanks. He smiled at her, and she leaned forward to kiss him gently. She loved him so much. All she wished for in that moment was that her sister could know such deep and true emotion.

"I'll talk to the mind healer, but I make no promises." Jana's assent was grudgingly given, but Jeri breathed a sigh of relief when she heard the small words.

Jana leaned back, her legs giving out as she let Darak scoop her up into his arms once more. He seated her on his lap again as if nothing had just happened, a satisfied smile on his face that didn't quite reach his eyes.

"So, what's planned for dinner? Just a few of us or the whole tribe?" Darak wanted to know, shifting the conversation to safer waters.

"Just immediate family, I thought." Micah looked at his chronometer.

"So, just part of the tribe." Darak nodded. "Good plan." He turned his face to Jana, sitting so patiently in his lap. "Are you up to meeting a few more family members tonight? I know they want to meet you. Nothing formal, just a family get-together."

"I have very little to wear but hospital jumpsuits and gowns."

"Not to worry. I've thought of everything." This was news to Jeri, and she aimed a curious glance over at her cousin-in-law. "I had a small selection of suitable clothing made for you while you were in the hospital and delivered to your suite here. Once we get you to your room, you should be able to find something to wear."

"That was very kind of you."

Jana seemed a bit overwhelmed, as well as perplexed, by his thoughtfulness. Jeri even thought she saw the beginning of a tear form in her sister's eye, and she realized that this was probably one of the few times in Jana's life that someone had anticipated her needs and given her an unexpected gift. Jeri vowed it wouldn't be the last.

Darak shrugged then lifted her in his arms as he stood from the seat. "Come on, I want to show you what I picked out. There's this little blue number that I think will look amazing on you with all those new blue sparklies in your skin."

He gave her an exaggerated wink and made for the door while she was still laughing. It lightened Jeri's heart to hear her sister's laughter, and she turned to her husband and hugged him tight.

"Do you think Darak and my sister…?"

"Yes?" Micah seemed to ponder the idea for a moment. "Well, stranger things have happened, and it's about time Dar settled down with a strong woman. Let's just hope she's not too strong for him." A frown creased his brow momentarily.

"I don't want to see him hurt."

She pushed at his shoulder. "I don't want Jana hurt any more either, but we can't protect them from everything, Micah. They need space to do this—or not—on their own. You can't protect Dar from every little thing like you have since you were kids. He needs to spread his wings and fly free from our influence for a bit. He needs to know he can."

Micah sighed. "You feel it, too? I should have known." He kissed her softly. "How did I rate such a wise and tender helpmate? I know Dar needs to find his own way, but I can't help wanting to protect him as I always have. I've always been the stronger of the pair of us. I'm older and supposedly wiser, right?"

"But he's a Master Mage now, Micah, and plenty strong in his own right. You may always be older, but just in this past hour, I've wondered if he's not wiser. The way he handled Jana is something I wouldn't have expected."

"Darak has a deep soul. His healing ability makes him more vulnerable to those in need, and your sister definitely qualifies. He already cares for her. We'll just have to wait and see if it develops into anything long lasting, or if she can return the feelings. She's been through a lot. It's amazing, really, that she's in as good shape as she is right now after all she's been through."

"The way you guided Darak? That's the way Jana guided me as we grew up. She's amazing, Micah. She just needs a little time to get back what the Wizards stole from her. Now that she's with us, I think she's got a good start on the road back. She used to be just as mischievous in her way as Darak is. It'll be good to see the teasing light come back into her eyes."

"Well, if anyone can do that, Darak can."

CHAPTER THREE

The clothes were gorgeous. The most beautiful things Jana had ever seen in her life. Darak had smiled as he told her to pick something out of the huge wardrobe that waited, and her jaw had dropped in sheer amazement.

"This is too much. I've never even seen this much clothing in one place, much less owned it."

"All the more reason for you to have a good selection from which to choose now." Darak went to the wardrobe and pulled out a shimmering blue creation of the softest shiffin fiber. It flowed over his arm in draping shimmers down to the floor. It was beautiful, as well as costly, she knew. "This is the one I was thinking about for tonight. Not too revealing, not too demure. Bold, yet classy, and you'll look amazing in it."

She allowed him to hold the confection of rare fabric up to her shoulders and had to admit it felt like heaven. The color was almost the exact shade of blue of the crystal that now pulsed in her skin. She peered into the wardrobe and noted a lot of garments in the very same hue. He had somehow intuitively known that she wanted to minimize the appearance of the stones that she would wear now forever. Camouflaging them with blue clothing was a good first step.

She turned to him and placed a gentle kiss on his cheek

that apparently took him completely by surprise.

"What was that for?"

She swallowed the tears that threatened before she could answer him.

"Thank you, Lord Darak." She cleared her throat softly before continuing. "This is the kindest thing anyone has ever done for me."

He moved in close, his thumb wiping the small tear that escaped her eye. The tenderness in his gaze was enough to break her heart.

"You deserve finery, Jana, and all the kindness we can give you. You've had a hard time with the Wizards and still have a long road of recovery ahead, but you need to know you're safe here with us. Safe, and welcome and treasured." He leaned down and placed a soft kiss on her trembling lips then pulled back as if it were the hardest thing he'd ever done. "Now, go try that on and let me bask in my largesse." He patted her butt lightly before settling on her bed and stretching his arms up to rest behind his head as he leaned back against the richly padded headboard.

She turned on shaky legs for the huge bathroom he had shown her earlier. And it was a real bathroom, with running water and a huge sunken tub, big enough for two. Having spent much of her time aboard ship, she wasn't used to bathing with water or having this much room in which to do it. This was a luxury she could all too easily come to require.

With a smile, she tugged off the hated hospital jumpsuit and pulled on the shimmering creation in blue. While it had never before been her favorite color, she was coming to appreciate the way this shade of almost-turquoise set off her eyes. The color made her come alive and lit her complexion as well as complementing and somewhat downplaying the sparkling gems that were now part of her very skin.

She looked damn good, and she knew it. It was an odd sensation. She had never before dressed to please a man, let alone herself. She was nervous about facing Darak and what she might see in his eyes. True, she was the older sister, but little Jeri seemed to know way more about pleasing a man than Jana ever would. Then again, she had never wanted to please a man—and wasn't sure she did now. She didn't want to have sex with anyone ever again, but she wanted Darak's approval. No, she *needed* his approval. Somehow, his opinion had become all-important to her, regardless of whether she could ever consider having sex with him or any other man. It wasn't about sex. It was about acceptance and... caring.

The very thought was mind boggling, but there it was. She wanted Darak to care for her...as she was coming to care for him. Amazing. She had not realized until this very moment that she was coming to feel something other than gratefulness to the big lug. True, he'd healed her and saved her life back on the *Circe* when she'd been so wounded, but she didn't remember much of that. She had been unconscious most of the time. But all those weeks in the hospital with him as her only visitor must have endeared him to her in some way without her even being aware of it.

Well, it couldn't continue. She had never cared for the opinion of a man—not since leaving home at least—and she wouldn't start now. Darak could say whatever he liked about her outfit, and it wouldn't matter in the least to her. She refused to let it.

That thought firmly in mind, she held her head high as she left the bathroom. He hadn't moved from his indolent pose on her spacious bed, and his eyes fairly caught fire when he saw her move into the room. He let out a low whistle of appreciation.

"You're stunning, Jana. Absolutely gorgeous."

* * *

With the confidence that Darak's reaction had given her, it was somewhat easier to walk on her stubbornly shaky legs into the formal dining area to meet the family. Darak was at her side, ready to catch her if she fell. It made it easier to walk on her own, just knowing he was there. His warm presence at her side also gave her courage to face this larger than expected group of strangers who all eyed her so assessingly.

"Don't let them scare you. They all defer to Micah and Jeri now, even if some of the old timers grumble about it."

"You're a rogue, Darak." Her whisper was meant for his ears alone, but the beautiful older woman who approached her seemed to have heard. She smiled widely.

"I have often despaired that my only son will always be a rogue, *dama*. I'm Darak's mother, Delila." She was taller than Jana and leaned down to kiss her cheek in welcome as Jana blushed.

"Forgive me, Lady Delila. I was only…"

"Speaking the truth?" Delila laughed gaily as she hugged her grown son briefly before turning back to Jana. "Darak is a rogue, a rake and a scoundrel, and I couldn't love him more. It's good that you have his number already. He won't be able to pull any tricks on you." The older woman winked audaciously at her. Delila tucked Jana's hand into her arm and guided her forward.

"I love you, too, Mother." Darak's droll reply made both women laugh as he followed close behind them.

Delila introduced Jana to Darak's father, a strongly built older man who looked a lot like his son with the same dark hair and twinkling eyes. He surprised her by greeting her with a kiss on the lips, which was repeated by nearly everyone in the room. She soon realized this was the normal greeting among these people, so different from the traditions of her own world.

Jana's head spun with all the names of the people she met. She saw the marked resemblance when Delila introduced Micah's parents and his sisters before finally seating Jana next to Jeri and moving to take her own seat between her son and husband. Darak was on Jana's other side, so his mother was only one seat away. Jeri, of course, sat beside her husband, and his family was next to him around the large table. Everyone was welcoming and friendly, and soon, conversation was flying as food was served in a seemingly never-ending stream from the kitchens.

Everything was just a bit overwhelming for her, but Darak was at her side, silently clasping her hand beneath the table when she felt particularly uncomfortable. Somehow, he always knew and took a moment to calm her with his strong and steady touch. Jeri did her best to make Jana feel comfortable, explaining all she could about the people and traditions of this strange new world and amusing her with stories about the assembled family.

She could tell they were all curious about her, but they were respectful of her, as well. None intruded or asked difficult questions. All seemed to want to make her feel welcome, though being in the center of such a large family was something she had never before experienced.

It was something she had always wanted. She could remember dimly the boisterous family dinners with her own mother and father, and little Jeri of course. They'd had a small family, but a happy one, and the horses had always been there, an extension of the family unit.

"Darak told me you brought the horses to these lands, Jeri."

Jeri leaned close, as if sharing a secret. "They are wonderful, Jana. They want to meet you."

"You can still talk to them?" Jana's voice was soft with wonder. Her little sister's gift was something she had always admired.

Jeri beamed. "More than ever. It was the horses that saved me on Mithrak. They hid me, and when they were sold off, I stowed away with them in the hold of the transport ship."

"Stars! Jeri, that was dangerous."

"It would have been worse to stay on Mithrak. You were long gone, and they knew I was hiding there somewhere. It was the only way." She shrugged. "It worked out. I ended up on Pantur with the Hill Tribes and worked with them as a horsetamer. That's how Micah found me." She tugged her husband's hand close, stroking his fingers with her own as he continued his conversation with his mother. The easy affection between them brought a pang of something like longing to Jana's heart as she watched.

"I thought Pantur was a psi null world."

Jeri nodded. "A perfect place to hide."

"But you would have stood out, even shielded."

"Not Jeri," Darak put in from her side. "She's the only Talent I've ever seen who can shield null."

Jana's eyes widened. "Truly?"

Jeri just nodded, blushing slightly. "I learned to do it out of necessity. That's why the Wizards could never find me."

"Amazing." Jana sighed and sat back, unable to eat another bite of the sumptuous meal.

"Would you like to meet the herd tomorrow afternoon?"

Jana thought about it for a moment. The horses were the last connection to her childhood. Perhaps they could bring her some measure of the peace that was eluding her. Slowly, she nodded.

"I think I'd like that."

A short time later, Darak deposited her in her suite, her legs having given out less than halfway to her rooms. He laid her gently on the bed, comming a maidservant to help her out of the blue confection and into an equally lovely sleeping gown he had pulled from her dresser. Before the servant arrived, he took his leave, draping the gown over the foot of her bed.

He seemed infinitely more gentle with her than he'd ever been before, and she didn't quite understand why, but was thankful for it. After the upheaval of the day, she couldn't have handled his usual roguish charm. He left her with a peck on the cheek and a promise that he was just down the hall if she needed him.

Her mind lingered on his thoughtfulness as she drifted off to sleep. Never had a man treated her so kindly and with so little encouragement. He knew full well by now that she would not agree to sex with him or any man, so he couldn't be after that. She guessed he could get sex from just about any woman he wanted simply by smiling at them and crooking his finger. Yet, what was it that caused him to be so kind to her? What was in it for him? She had no idea, but the thought plagued her. It just didn't make sense.

The next day, she felt much better, her legs starting the day, at least, fully functional. Jeri bounded into her room after a perfunctory knock with the same youthful enthusiasm she'd had when they were girls. She bounced on the edge of the huge bed until Jana threw a pillow at her, and they both giggled. Jeri found an outfit suitable for riding in the magical wardrobe. It seemed Darak had forgotten nothing when it came to dressing her for all occasions.

Jana went to the bathroom to change at Jeri's urging and came out dressed in sleek dark blue that complemented her hair.

"We're not visiting the herd until this afternoon, but you look lovely in that outfit, Jan."

"It's good for riding, but it seems like it could be worn for other occasions, as well."

Jeri nodded as she smoothed the collar in back. "It's a versatile design. I had one made almost exactly like this a few weeks ago." She smiled archly. "Now, I know where Darak ordered at least part of your wardrobe from, the sneaky man. He really outfitted you well, Jan. I'm amazed at what he managed to get for you in such a short time. He must've begun ordering this collection when you first arrived in the hospital." Jeri shook her head in wonder. "Who knew the man had such good taste?"

After a private breakfast with her sister, Jana was escorted to a small, sunny chamber that overlooked the extensive gardens on the south side of the compound. A gray bearded old man sat there, waiting for her, it seemed. Jeri pushed her into the room in front of her when she slowed, a patient smile on her face.

"Jana, this is Master Toombs. He is the mind healer we talked about yesterday. Micah and I asked him to come see you."

Jana nodded grimly. "I know it must be done, but you

should understand that I'm not looking forward to this." She addressed the older man directly.

He stood politely, smiling benevolently at the two women. "*Dama*, that is a healthy attitude, and I value your honesty with both me and yourself. You have already taken the first step."

"Thank you for coming, Master Toombs. I know this was short notice."

He turned to Jeri, gifting her with a wide smile. "Sha Jeri, I am glad to be of service to you in any way. You have only to comm me. Any time."

Jana realized in that moment that being a Sha apparently had some benefits if Mage Masters jumped to your beck and call. But her little sister seemed to be handling her new celebrity status well, still grounded and humble. She was a good kid who had grown into a remarkable woman. Jana squeezed her hand as Jeri took her leave.

"I love you, Jana."

"I love you, too, little sis."

The session wasn't easy, but it was a good start. The Mage Master with the incredibly strong mind healing Talent was calm and gentle when examining her worst memories, non-judgmental and kind. Mind healing wasn't just his Talent; she could easily tell it was his calling. He helped her remember and put behind her just a few of the many horrific things that had been done to her under the collective's control. They would require many more sessions like this one before all the trauma was dealt with, but already she felt freer than she had just an hour before.

She left the older man with a smile and a deep nod of thanks and respect. She knew he already appreciated the satisfaction she felt with the work they had done that morning. He was, after all, a Mage Master with the ability to delve into her deepest thoughts and memories.

"How did it go?"

She shouldn't have been surprised to find Darak waiting on the other side of the door for her, but he startled her nonetheless. She closed her eyes briefly, still facing the door, to collect her thoughts, then turned toward him.

"It went well." She began to walk, and he fell into step beside her. "I'm meeting with him again tomorrow morning and for the next week, at least."

"Toombs is a good man. One of the most revered of all Mage Masters."

She could hear respect and even a little awe in his voice. "Aren't you also a Mage Master?"

Darak surprised her by laughing. "Yeah, I guess I am, but it's still so new, I don't really feel as if I'm even close to his league. I jumped right past Mage from Dominar, so I feel a little like I cheated."

She knew his great leap in strength was because of her. When the crystal in her control scepter had exploded, the wash of residual power had affected all the crew of the *Circe* in unexpected ways. She felt a bit like it was her fault, still.

She stopped in her tracks and turned to face him in the long hall. "I've come to think that things happen as they do for a reason. It's the only way I can accept all that was done to me. I like to think that the Wizards got me so they'd leave Jeri free, and look how that ended up. She's grown to be a fierce woman with more power than I ever could have imagined and a husband who loves her deeply."

"I'm glad you realize that." Darak looked uncomfortable for a short moment. "Micah loves her more than life. I love her, too, but not in the same way. I've never loved any woman like that." He ran one hand through his hair. "I love her for what she did for my cousin and the joy she's brought to all of us. He was so unhappy before he found her. She's brought renewed meaning to his life. She's given hope to all the Council worlds and freedom to you, as well as several hundred others who were once under the control of the collective. She is an amazing woman, and in you, I see her origins. You can be just as amazing, Jana, but you have to heal first."

He turned away, leaving her stunned. She'd read such

passion in his eyes, such caring, such hope. All for her. It left her shaky, and this time, it wasn't from any weakness in her muscles, but from sheer emotional awe.

She followed as he led down the hall toward a small dining room where they would meet Jeri and Micah for an early lunch before going down to see the horses. They came around a corner, and Jana stopped dead in her tracks.

Two young men were there, naked, their hard cocks inside the same small maidservant who had helped Jana so meekly into her nightgown the night before. Shill was her name, she recalled, but she didn't know the two young men, and she barely recognized the look of ecstasy on the young maid's face as she urged her lovers to move harder and deeper inside her ass and pussy. One driving in while the other pulled out, over and over.

Darak moved to stand beside Jana, sliding his arm around her shoulders, pinning her in place when she would have retreated. She was forced to watch, but truly, she couldn't take her eyes off the scene down the corridor. It was obvious the whole thing was consensual, totally unlike any of her own sexual encounters. The maid was begging for the men to take her, to make her come. It was obvious she wanted every moment of this.

"Do you like what you see?" Darak breathed in her ear, his arm holding her captive. "Have you ever thought of having two men at once?"

Jana shook her head almost violently.

"Not even when you realized Micah and I shared your sister, much as Kirt and Whelan are doing with Shill now? Don't tell me you didn't wonder what she felt, what *we* felt. I won't believe you."

"I don't want that. I don't want any man." She shivered, and he pulled her back against his chest.

"I'm sorry, baby." He turned her in his arms and hugged her close, hiding her eyes in his muscled chest. "I know you don't think you want to ever have sex again, but you will. One day, you will. And, on that day, I want you to think of me. I want it to be me, Jana. I want to be the man inside you—the man you *want* inside you. I want to be the man to give you pleasure like you've never had before."

It was all too much for Jana. Her whole body trembled as the maid screamed in orgasm behind her. She heard two male groans, and then, Darak swung her up into his arms, carrying her past the threesome and on into another hall, away from where they'd meant to go.

"What about lunch?" She made a token protest, though, in truth, she was too shaken to even think about eating or making light conversation with her sister and Micah.

"We've got time, yet."

Darak's voice was gruff as he shouldered open a large door, moving swiftly until she felt a soft surface beneath her back. She looked around and realized immediately that she was in a bedroom, and the soft surface was a huge, darkly draped bed. It was a masculine room, probably Darak's own, she realized in one corner of her mind.

"Why did you bring me here?"

"Do you like the room?" Darak was seated near her, but not touching as he casually unfastened his shirt. Her eyes grew wide as his hard muscled chest came into view between the parting cloth. "Burgundy has always been one of my favorite colors, though, just recently, I've formed a fondness for blue."

Her mouth went dry as his eyes sizzled a path from the blue jewels in her face, down her neck and over the myriad stones they both knew sparkled in the skin over her breasts and lower. She blinked, trying to focus, but that only brought his masculine perfection into sharper focus as he shrugged out of his shirt. He sat there, facing her, still as a statue in every way but for his eyes. They met hers with gentle patience, a hint of longing and something she could have sworn was caring, but didn't quite dare believe.

"I talked to Master Toombs before your session this morning. He won't ever betray your confidences, but he agreed to teach me a bit about the usual paths of recovery from something like what happened to you."

"Why?" That seemed the all-important question at the moment, though she could barely form the single word. Darak moved closer, touching the sparkling gems on her cheek softly, his gaze tracing the curves of her face.

"I don't want to scare you or rush you. I…care for you, Jana, in a way I never expected. I want to help you overcome your past and make peace with your present."

"That's a very tall order, Darak."

Her eyes shifted away as he came nearer. His big arms surrounded her lightly, his warm skin a comfort to her. He held her loosely, protectively almost, though there was a banked fire in his eyes.

"What you saw in the hall—that was perfectly normal for people on Council worlds. I know you were shocked, maybe even a little appalled, but joining with others is something we almost take for granted. Those two young men are cousins of mine, and they both have strong, though fledgling, Talents. Joining with Shill in that way reenergizes them, and she is more than happy to be part of their therapy."

"Reenergizes them? In what way?"

He rested his chin atop her head, tugging her closer as her breathing slowed a bit. Little by little, it seemed he was acclimating her to his touch. The sneaky bastard.

"Kirt and Whelan have been assigned study sessions in the mornings. I know this because they were part of the crew of the *Circe* on our last run, and they, too, leapt up a bit in the rankings after Micah and Jeri freed you from the collective. They're young, just yeomen on their first voyages, and now, suddenly they have to deal with a whole lot of new energy they never expected. My uncle Brandon has been working with them, when he has time, and he is a harsh taskmaster. He trained Micah and I in our early years, and we often needed frequent replenishment of our energies after a session with him." He chuckled, and she felt it all the way through her body, pressed as she was against him now. "Sex is one of the most powerful, and pleasurable, ways to recharge our psi batteries, so to speak. The first time your sister and her mate took pity on me and allowed me to share pleasure with them was, in fact, just after we'd all three spent all our energy to try to heal one small boy on the planet Liata."

"I don't want to hear about you and my sister." Anger bubbled up at the thought of them together. Anger and, loath as she was to admit it, jealousy.

His big hands stroked her back soothingly. "I understand that better than you think, but you must know the truth of it so doubt cannot stand between us. At least that's what Master Toombs told me, and I think his words have merit. You need to know that it wasn't done lightly or without good reason. We were in a combat situation and needed to return to full strength quickly so we could help the people of Liata. The stakes were high, and we did what we had to do." He chuckled once more, squeezing her lightly. "Not that we didn't enjoy it."

She punched him on the arm. "You're a rogue." Then, she thought about Liata—the planet against which she had led an invasion force while still under the control of the collective. The guilt tore at her soul. "Did you save the boy?"

"Yes. You'll meet him no doubt, in time. He is the youngest brother of the *Circe's* Loadmaster, Trini."

"I'm glad."

She sighed, and her breath caused a shiver in him, she noted. She wasn't sure if she liked the idea that she could cause him any sort of sexual response. She knew men when they were out of control sexually, and she didn't dare think of what damage this huge male could do to her if he should lose control.

She tried to back away from him, but his arms tightened. He wouldn't let her go, and she began to panic.

"Darak, I don't want this."

He stroked her back in long motions, murmuring softly. "Be at ease, sweet Jana. I only want to hold you. That's all. To feel you against my skin and know you are with me."

"I won't have sex with you."

He chuckled. "I know. You're not ready for that yet, but one day... One day, you will be, and I'll be with you. I dream of that day, Jana. Every night since I met you, I dream of the day you'll be mine."

The thought of it scared her, but yet, his raspy words caused a shiver of something like fire deep down in her womb. It was the oddest sensation, and she didn't understand it at all. He made her feel all quivery, and not from weakness, but from some sort of female power she never knew she had.

"I don't think that day will ever come. Not for you or any man, Darak." Her words were much softer than she intended and laced with something that sounded awfully like regret.

Darak pulled back slightly, and his gaze zeroed in on her lips. Telegraphing his intentions, he leaned in slowly, but she couldn't move. She was paralyzed, waiting for his inevitable kiss. She didn't know why she wanted it, but she did.

His lips met hers gently at first, then with tender pressure. His hot tongue swept inside, stroking her with his masculine heat. She heard a moan and realized dimly that it came from her own throat as his pressure increased and he moved her closer to his body.

At some point, he began unfastening her clothing, but she didn't notice until suddenly her bare nipples scraped his muscular chest. The sensation was like nothing she'd ever felt before. It was heavenly!

He was sculpted and firm, yet gentle and somehow kind. He touched her so tenderly, was so careful of her, she could hardly equate this ultra sexual touching with the kind of assault she had experienced before. Darak was truly a master at giving pleasure. Perhaps, she thought with one small, cautious part of her brain that was still functioning, she would follow where this led and find out if she could truly experience the kind of pleasure of which he and her sister had spoken. Could it be possible?

She was shocked out of her incredible thoughts by his fingers closing around her nipple. He tugged firmly, igniting a fire in her womb that was new and exciting. She squirmed underneath him as he guided her down to lie on her back on the firm mattress. He was hot and hard above her, his chest rubbing rhythmically against hers as his hands traced paths over her skin, lingering on the still healing crystal invasions, zapping her with little jolts of his energy even as his caresses inflamed her senses. Even in passion, he was mindful of her healing body and tried to help her. She realized, in that moment, that this remarkable man was more than the roguish exterior he tried so hard to cultivate, truly.

"Darak," she moaned when he let her up for air, "what are you doing to me?"

He kissed his way down her throat, his lips moist and firm against her skin.

"Pleasuring you, sweet Jana."

His voice rumbled against the side of her breast before his mouth opened over her nipple, sucking it in deep. She nearly shot off the bed, the pleasure was so intense. While he sucked, his hands roamed. One inserted itself into the opening of her wide slacks, pushing down and in until he reached her unbelievably wet pussy.

"Mmm." He pulled back from her nipple with a wet popping sound and smiled down at her. "You're wet for me. I think you like this more than you thought you would. Am I right?"

Confusion reigned in her mind for a moment, but she couldn't deny the pleasure zinging through her veins. She nodded, her eyes wide as his mouth moved to her other nipple and his hand pushed farther between her legs.

"Open for me, Jana. Spread your legs and let me show you how it can be."

She complied without conscious thought as he bit down gently with his perfect, white teeth on her other nipple, the one with the crystal shards arrayed around it in a semi-circular pattern. Was it her imagination or were the crystals pulsing in time with his tongue's pulling on her nipple? The thought made her even hotter.

And then, his fingers found her clit. He rubbed and

teased, finally pushing one of his long, strong fingers down into her hole, sliding deep and easily through the copious wetness there for him. She couldn't help it, she screamed when her body exploded in pleasure, calling his name.

It was long moments before she could open her eyes. Her breath came in rough pants as he leaned over her, placing little nipping kisses all over her bare chest. She was amazed to realize she still wore her loosened slacks and his hand rested over her pussy as if soothing his favorite pet.

"You're beautiful when you come." His devilish eyes twinkled down at her as she blushed to the roots of her hair.

"I… I've never done that... I've never felt that before." Her words were hesitant, her mind still unable to grasp the enormity of what had just happened.

"Then, I'm truly blessed." His words were formal, his tone serious as he leaned forward to kiss her. "I'm honored to be the one to teach you first of pleasure. Thank you for sharing that with me." He pulled his hand out of her crotch and brought it to his lips, igniting her fire all over again as he licked his fingers quite deliberately. "You taste divine, as well, Jana." His eyes held promises. "I would very much like to lick you there one day soon. I hope you'll let me."

"Darak!" She was completely scandalized as he chuckled at her response.

"Now, tell me. Don't you feel a bit more energized than you did just a few moments ago? Even that little act of pleasure can bring you a great reserve of energy. Do you feel it?"

Jana thought about how she felt, physically and psychically, and she realized with a start that her low energy reserves had been recharged to some extent in just these few short moments. It was amazing, really. Such a small thing to bring so much energy. She would have had to spend weeks resting to regain these levels that came from just one orgasm in Darak's capable arms. No wonder these Talents shared their bodies so freely if this was the result. She began to understand a little bit about why these people had evolved to behave as scandalously as they did and how her little sister could have come to accept such behavior when they had been raised quite differently.

"I do feel better." She couldn't keep the surprise from her voice, and he lifted her to a sitting position with a lusty grin.

"Feel free to call on me any time you need a boost, Jana. I mean that sincerely."

"I'll just bet you do." She was amazed she felt free enough to tease him, and his answering rakish smile warmed her heart.

"Now, much as I enjoy these," he cupped her breasts in his large hands, squeezing gently and rubbing her nipples until she squirmed, "we're late for lunch."

"Stars! I forgot."

He laughed out loud while she scrambled back into her top before shoving his shirt into his hands and urging him to get dressed. If he didn't get that stupid grin off his face, Jeri and her mate would know exactly what had held them up. That stupid grin, and the raging erection she saw outlined quite clearly as he stood in front of her to tuck in his shirttails.

Suddenly, she felt guilty. She was no better than the demon men who had raped her and left her wanting while she'd been under the Wizards' control. She'd taken all the pleasure here and given Darak nothing.

"I'm sorry." Her words whispered through the room, stopping his laughter. He dropped to one knee in front of her, taking her shoulders gently in his hands as he sought her eyes.

"For what?"

"You gave me something here, Darak, and I've given you nothing. I don't think I even can." Her doubts swamped her, but his arms reassured her as he pulled her close for a quick hug.

"I ask for nothing but your happiness, Jana. This isn't a competition, and I'm not keeping score. I consider it a privilege to give you pleasure, and I ask nothing in return.

Not now. Perhaps not ever, if you cannot put your past behind you. Allow me to help you, Jana. Allow me to bring you pleasure when you need it. That's all I want."

A tear shimmered down her face. This man was too amazing for words. She feared he would grow tired of his promise, but then, he'd already seen her through so many weeks of therapy in the hospital. He was a good man who lived up to his promises, she could tell.

"It seems so unfair." She pushed back from his embrace and wiped her face. "You're a very special man, Darak of Geneth Mar. More special than I deserve."

He kissed her lightly, almost as if in benediction, before rising and holding out his hand to help her stand. He had led her almost to the door before he spoke.

"You deserve all that is good and pure in this world, Jana, but for now, I guess you'll have to settle for me. Slightly tarnished and ragged from overuse, but still willing to try."

She laughed at his self-assessment as they left the chamber, and he kept her laughing all the way to the luncheon room.

CHAPTER FOUR

Micah and Jeri weren't oblivious to the blush on Jana's cheeks or the twinkle in Darak's eyes, not to mention the bulge in his pants, but they said nothing to make Jana feel even more uncomfortable as they sat down to a light lunch. Before long, the conversation turned to the herd of horses that had been brought together in one of the larger expanses of open land that was part of the massive estate.

Jeri told her sister how she had sent out a silent call to those wild horses in the area that wanted to come live free on their land and how, only a few days later, a large herd had gathered. There were untamed lands and mountains off to the west of the estate, where most of the horses had carved out a living for themselves. They would still roam free, but if they needed any sort of help, be it food or water or medical assistance, they now had a refuge. Jeri and the staff of capable horsemen she had chosen and was training would see to it that her promise to the wild horses of Geneth Mar was kept.

"You can still speak with the horses." Jana's voice was full of pride and a bit of awe as she regarded her little sister. "Papa had the same gift."

"Did he?" Jeri was excited by the idea that her gift had been passed down from her lost parent.

Jana frowned slightly. "He never spoke of it with you? I

mean, I know it was his big secret, but when I turned thirteen, he sat me down and told me about his gift. He taught me how to shield my own fledgling powers and warned me never to speak of them to anyone but him or Mother."

"They both died before I turned thirteen." Jeri's voice held aching sadness, and Jana held her hand out to her sister, an offer of comfort.

"I remember his words, Jer. I'll tell you what he told me." Both women were fighting back tears. "Papa said that I should embrace my gift and not fear it, but rather fear the Wizards that would try to use me for my gift. He said he and Mama had lived in fear of the Wizards their whole life, but by being careful and shielding tight, they had survived so far. He warned me to do the same, but above all, he told me to be happy. As he was with Mama and us."

"Little did he know we would have so little time left with our family." Jeri's face was sad, her eyes wistful. "He was such a good man."

Tears rolled down her face, and the two girls clung to each other, the men placing their broad hands on the women's backs in silent comfort.

Before long, they all decided to troop outside and see the horses. The herds had always been a source of peace for Jeri, and Jana remembered her time among the horses of their homeworld with fondness, though she hadn't been around horses in many years. Jana was tentative, at first, her wobbly legs unsure on the uneven turf, her gait uncertain as the huge animals bore down on them. Jeri, of course, was fearless, holding up her arms to the big stallion that galloped over to receive her attention first. Jeri's laughter rang out through the countryside and lightened every heart that heard it.

Jana remembered her childhood spent among the herds on Mithrak as several of the young colts and fillies gathered around her, tickling her with their velvety muzzles. She reached out to them with her hands and her unshielded mind, surprised when she received a few faint images of happiness and warmth from their complex minds.

"Jeri!"

Suddenly, a huge black stallion moved his way through the smaller horses, vying for Jana's attention, and stopped just in front of her, eyeing her carefully. Jana held her breath. This was, by far, the most gorgeous animal she had ever beheld, and he seemed to know it. He was haughty and powerful, sizing her up as she regarded him.

"I call him Darkest Hour." Jeri's soft voice came from not too far away. Jana knew her sister was watching them, but she couldn't tear her eyes from the great stallion that faced her. "He is the leader of the wild band from the western mountains. The yearlings are all his get."

Jana could see it then, the remarkable resemblance between this strong stallion and the young horses that had so playfully greeted her. They had his strong shoulders and powerful build, though none had a match for his pure black, glossy coat.

"He's magnificent." Jana's voice was a mere breath of sound. The stallion stamped his foot once as if in agreement and bowed his head just slightly. She took that as a sign that she could move closer. She wanted to touch this beautiful, powerful creature. She wanted to commune with him on a non-verbal level.

She reached out her hand, and he moved into her caress, fitting his soft cheek into the palm of her hand. She smiled and stroked him, patting gently and scratching by his ears as he moved into her. Within moments, she found herself putting her arms around his strong neck, his huge head moving to encapsulate her in his warmth and seeming protection. It was a moment of pure magic.

Without conscious thought, she stroked her fingers into his thick mane and, with an agility she'd thought long gone, she pulled herself up onto his bare back. She was breathless a moment, waiting to see if he would let her ride, and then, he was off, slowly at first until he cleared the crowd of the herd and people, then faster and faster as she found her seat. She felt as if she had never been away from the horses with which she'd been raised. She felt a perfect union with the glorious beast beneath her as he picked up speed across the open field.

She heard the pounding of hooves just behind her and realized that her sister followed on a powerful mare, keeping pace, there for Jana if she should need her, much as their papa had done when they were little. It made her feel warm and protected in a way she hadn't felt since the Wizards had ripped her from her home.

Tears streamed down her face and into the wind, but it was a cleansing feeling that claimed her when Darkest Hour finally came to a stop at her urging. She would have liked to ride all day and all night, but her legs were just too weak. She was trembling from head to toe when the horse walked back to the waiting men. Darak's eyes were filled with pride, and his smile spoke of the care she had only just realized lay between them. When the stallion stopped beside him, she tumbled down into his arms, allowing him to guide her and support her weak body with absolute trust.

He carried her back to her room where she promptly fell into a deep, healing sleep. She didn't awaken until just before dinner when Shill, the maid, came to help her prepare.

* * *

The days went on in much the same way for a few weeks. Each morning, she would meet with Master Toombs, and little by little, she was putting her past behind her. Darak continued to be a nearly constant presence, though he didn't push her any further than he had that first day at the estate. She rode the horses and formed a deep bond with the magnificent stallion who remained nearby, seemingly waiting for her whenever she set foot outdoors. She was regaining her strength quickly, surrounded by the love and acceptance of her sister, but she knew others still harbored doubts about her.

"I won't be here for the next few days. I have to go up to

the *Circe* and oversee the refit." Darak's voice cut through the dinnertime chatter, startling her.

"How is it coming along?" Micah wanted to know, lifting his goblet and failing to not look too interested in the fate of his old ship.

"The repairs were completed this morning, and the new bits are going to be installed starting tomorrow. Which is why I want to be there."

Micah nodded. "Understandable. When do they want you to go back out?"

"You mean you don't know?" Darak grinned at his powerful cousin. "I thought it was you that had put me on hold."

"Hold?" Jeri entered the conversation. "We didn't know, Dar. I swear. I wonder why they'd hold the *Circe* back?"

"I don't know," Micah's eyes turned speculative, "but it could have something to do with the comm I received just before dinner. I was going to wait until we were finished eating, but you might as well know now. The Council wants to question Jana next week. They say they've waited long enough."

"Micah! You've got to do something."

"No, Jeri." Jana finally spoke up. "I expected to be interrogated sooner or later. I'd just as soon get it over with."

"But you're not strong enough, yet."

Jana held up her hand, calming her volatile sister. "I'm as good as I'm going to get, for now. I need to talk to them and tell them what little I know." She sighed. "I just want to put it behind me as soon as possible and get on with my life."

Darak surprised her by taking her hand and squeezing, catching her eyes with his concerned expression. "I'll go with you, Jana. You don't have to face them alone."

"And they'll treat you with respect," Micah assured her. "If they get out of line, they know they'll have Jeri and me on their case."

Jana smiled. "You are all too good to me. With such allies, what do I have to fear?" She took a sip of her wine, taking her hand back from Darak. She wouldn't let them see just how frightened she was at the prospect of the interrogation to come.

The days Darak was away from the estate dragged. Jana didn't realize until he left just how used to his hulking presence she'd become. It was like a piece of her was missing when he wasn't around.

But he came home—she'd come to think of the place as home in even such a short time—just before she was due to leave for the Council compound. She was rising when a perfunctory knock sounded on her bedchamber door. Before she could answer, the door swung inward, and Darak was there.

He was a sight for sore eyes, though she would never let him know it.

"Isn't it customary to wait to be invited in?"

"If I waited for an invitation, sweetheart, I'd grow old before my time."

"You got that right," she muttered as she tied the sash on her robe a bit tighter. "I could have been dressing."

"One can only wish." His devilish smile softened her stance a bit. The rogue had a charm about him that was hard to resist. "You're looking better all the time, Jana. How do you feel?"

"Stronger. More fit." She moved to the window to look out over the western fields where the horses roamed free. "Riding again has helped a lot. My legs are stronger each day."

"And what of the crystals?" He'd come up behind her without making a sound, but now, his voice drifted down over her like a caress, so close did he stand behind her. "Do they still burn?" His fingers grazed the crystals in her cheek, tendrils of his gentle healing energy zapping into her with an exciting caress.

"I'm getting used to them, and they to me, it seems. My body is starting to be able to regulate their power flow a bit— or so the med techs tell me."

"That's good." His hand slid down over her right side, caressing and sending healing energy to the myriad shards nestled into her skin under the soft fabric of her robe.

"You don't have to spend your energy on me, Dar. It really doesn't hurt that much, anymore."

He pulled her lightly back against his chest, enveloping her in his warmth. "Any pain is too much, Jana, when I can do something about it. I don't like to see you hurting."

She remained silent as he sent even more energy into her skin, soothing hurts she hadn't even realized were there. She let him do it, knowing somehow that he derived a deep satisfaction from using his healing powers. She wouldn't let him drain himself, however, but he stopped long before his massive reserves of energy were even tapped.

He moved back, releasing her, much to her surprise. She turned and found him nearby, holding a length of soft, pale blue fabric in his rough hands.

"What is that?"

"A gift." He held it out and the material slithered between his fingers. It looked expensive.

"Not more clothes. Darak, you've already been way too generous. I will never be able to repay you at this rate."

"I expect no repayment. The clothes were gifts. But this..." he held up the odd creation as if presenting a masterpiece, "...is something special. I had it designed just for today."

"I meet with the Council today." She swallowed nervously.

He nodded, his eyes as serious as she'd ever seen them. "They will want to see the crystals."

"I thought as much." She blushed at the thought of so many eyes on her bare body.

Darak moved a step closer, holding the strange garment before him. "I know you were raised to be modest. I had this made so you could keep some of your modesty and still allow easy viewing of the crystals in your skin. Won't you at least try it on?"

"You did that for me?"

She was touched beyond words. She'd thought he least of all would worry over her discomfort with showing her naked body to strangers. They were so free on this planet, as she'd learned the hard way, having walked in upon multiple couplings in the past days between all sorts of people who lived on the large estate. She wouldn't have thought he would worry over her foreign sensibilities, but apparently, he did. Wonder of wonders. He had actually thought ahead to what the interrogation by the Council would mean to her. The idea left her momentarily speechless.

He moved closer. "Try it on. Please?"

Tears in her eyes, she took the slinky garment from his fingers. She held it between them for a long moment, questions in her eyes that he seemingly didn't want to answer.

Without speaking, he turned her by the shoulders and patted her butt to get her moving toward the bathroom. She went, as if in a daze. She closed the door and spent more than a few minutes trying to figure out how the odd garment was supposed to be put on. She got it eventually, after a few false starts, and what she saw in the mirror floored her.

The gown was modestly cut, except for the huge swaths cut out all along her right side, where the majority of the crystals sparkled in her skin. The clever drape of shimmersilk covered the strategic points of her nipples and the apex of her thighs, but each and every crystal shard was clearly visible, exposed to the air and the hungry gaze of the man standing behind her in the bathroom.

This time, he hadn't even knocked on the door before invading her space.

"It shows them all." She said the first thing that popped into her mind.

"To great advantage." His eyes sparkled, and the focus of his gaze on her body turned her insides to mush. "You'll probably start a whole new fashion trend once a few people see you in this."

"It's so formfitting, though..."

She was uncomfortable showing this much skin. Darak

moved closer, and his warm hands skimmed her midriff, just below her breasts. She didn't object as he pulled her back against his hard chest. Her eyes were glued to their reflections in the large mirror.

"It's either this or expose your lovely nipples to every member of the Council. Which would you rather do?" His hand lingered under the exposed curve of her right breast, rubbing over the stones permanently set in her soft flesh. He traced the fine web of shimmersilk that held the dress in place over her hardening nipple.

"Darak." Her voice was nothing more than a shocked whisper as he let his fingers roam under the gossamer fabric, stroking and touching, pinching and teasing.

"You're beautiful, Jana. Just let me touch you. That's all I want. Just to touch you." His voice was ragged as he turned her in his arms. His tortured gaze said even more than his words. "I dream of that day in your room when you came apart in my arms. I lie in bed at night and stroke myself, thinking of how you looked, how you sounded, how you tasted. I want to taste you again."

His lips moved toward hers slowly, with great deliberation. She knew he meant to kiss her, but she didn't turn away. She wanted it, too. She dreamed of him in the dark of night and, sometimes, even during the day. She dreamed of the pleasure he had shown her, knowing she had never felt such fierce passion before and never would again, if not with him.

Darak was the only man she could imagine letting this close to her. She worked daily with Master Toombs, but even that revered gentleman was unsure if she'd be able to have a normal sex life after what she'd been through.

Still, she wanted to try. With Darak. Only with him.

But she was scared.

His kiss started gently but soon escalated. His body bracketed hers, moving her toward the marble vanity table along one wall. She went willingly. So far, he hadn't done anything she didn't like. She had to warn him, though. Just in case.

"Darak," she whispered. "I'm not sure I can—"

He silenced her with his mouth, kissing her deeply enough that she forgot what she was going to say. So deeply, she forgot her own name.

"This is for you, sweet Jana." His raspy whisper was spoken against her lips as he let go for just a moment, only to hoist her upward to sit on the edge of the vanity. His hard body insinuated itself between her splayed legs, the shimmersilk of the gown flexing and stretching to give him all the room he wanted.

The part along the right side of the gown extended to her waist, allowing easy access. She hadn't been able to wear anything under the gown, and she gasped as she realized she was naked to his gaze when he dropped to his knees in front of her.

Strong hands pushed the expensive fabric upward and to her left, letting it pool on the vanity at her side. He guided her right leg upward so that her knee bent, making even more room for him. She could feel the heat a blush forming all over her body. There was an underlying heat, as well. A heat generated by Darak's touch, by his gaze as he examined her folds, by his tongue when he licked his lips.

"I'm going to eat you up, milady. And you're going to love it. I promise."

He didn't give her a chance to respond. His fingers stroked up her bare thighs and combed through the light curls over her mound. Then, they spread her wide, tracing the hidden contours of her pussy, touching places that had never been touched so carefully by a man before. He took exquisite care of her, never grabbing, never being too rough. Nothing about his behavior to this point reminded her of anything that had come before with men.

She could barely think as his finger found a little button of pleasure at the top of her thighs. It was something she'd heard about, but never experienced before Darak. He had a way of pulling responses out of her abused body that made her heart sing and her female parts shudder with pleasure.

She felt moisture releasing from that lonely part of her and tried to shut her thighs in embarrassment, but Darak soothed her.

"That's what I was waiting for." His voice was rough, his attention focused on her most private place. "You cream so beautifully for me, Jana. I want to taste your heat, your passion. I want to give you more pleasure than you can handle and feel you come apart in my arms." His gaze sought hers, and she read the truth of his words in his eyes. He wanted to give to her, asking nothing in return. He...cared?...for her on some level that she didn't understand. Just as she felt something inside her shielded heart for him. Something she didn't dare examine or name.

He held her gaze as one finger pressed into her core. Slowly...so slowly it made her squirm to get closer. She wanted more of his invasion. More of his possession. Though she'd never wanted any man inside her body before. Not even in this small way.

Darak pressed forward, his finger impaling her with its hard, flexible heat, bringing her a feeling she couldn't describe.

Then, he crooked his finger.

An explosion went off inside her as he touched some previously unknown hidden nerve endings that lit her up like a skyrocket. She jumped, and his lips widened into the most devilish grin he'd yet given her.

"You like that, don't you?" He did it again, and she nearly whimpered. "Oh, yes. I can see that you do." He teased her, beginning to stroke his long finger in and out of her channel, the way made easier by the moisture that continued to flow in small increments. Every third or fourth stroke, he'd add that little rub of his fingertip over the spot that made her squirm.

"Darak!" She was growing increasingly desperate for the release she'd only ever known in his arms. She reached for him, clutching his strong shoulders in silent entreaty.

"Do you want me to kiss you, *dama*?" His use of the honorific drew her gaze back to his. He stilled, waiting for an answer.

What was the question? It took her a moment to focus her scattered wits.

"I want..." What were the words to explain what she wanted more than life at this moment?

"Yes, *dama*? Your wish is my command." He had the audacity to wink at her.

How could he tease at a time like this? He had his finger up her cunt, her body writhing to his every movement, and the rogue had the nerve to take the time to tease her.

"I want to come, Darak. Please, make me come."

He withdrew his finger and sat back. She wanted to cry.

"All in good time."

He stroked her right foot, positioned on the edge of the vanity. How she'd ended up in such an indecorous position, she really had no idea. She tried to move, but he wouldn't let her.

He rose on his knees to kiss her foot, sucking each toe into his mouth. At first, it seemed a strange thing to do, but the way he held her gaze as he laved the sensitive skin between her toes made her realize there were erogenous places even there, where she least expected them.

Darak kissed his way up her calf to the bend of her knee and then down the other side, over the inside of her thigh. He nibbled and licked, nipped and even bit her gently a time or two, leaving no outward mark. Inwardly, she was on fire.

When he reached the place where her thigh met the rest of her body, he sat back to look again. His fingers returned to her folds, spreading them and rubbing over her clit with slow, steady, repetitive pressure until she was nearing the peak once more.

"Some people call these the nether lips," Darak mused, shocking her.

His contemplation of her body at such a critical time was maddening. Why did he talk so much? Why didn't he just let her come already? He really was the worst possible tease. He got her all hot and bothered—a state she had only ever achieved with him—then made her wait.

"I don't care what it's called," she muttered, contemplating ways to murder him in his sleep. He had the nerve to chuckle, which didn't help her mood.

"Oh, but you should, *dama*." He moved closer, inhaling her scent. He seemed pleasantly enthralled by his study of her, so she didn't feel too self-conscious.

"Why?" she felt compelled to ask.

"Because, wherever you have lips, I will always want to kiss them." So saying, his mouth lowered to her, delivering a kind of kiss she had never imagined. His tongue swirled through her folds, exciting the already engorged nub. He paused there to suck it into his mouth and tease her with his teeth and tongue. Then, he moved lower. His talented tongue delved inside her sheath, stroking as his finger had done, only thicker, hotter and wetter. The combination was enough to make her backside lift from the vanity as her body strained toward him.

His arms went around her, steadying her on her precarious perch. His mouth rode her as her pleasure peaked, riding her body in waves. She cried out as ecstasy hit her. It could have been his name she called, but she wasn't sure. It didn't matter. All that mattered was the man between her thighs and the pleasure only he had ever given her.

This climax was more than the one she'd had before. More demanding of her body and soul. More pleasurable than anything she had ever experienced. Longer and deeper than anything she could have imagined. She began to understand how people could seek out this kind of feeling again and again.

She was discovering how sex with one special man could become an addiction that would take a lifetime to fulfill.

"That's it, baby. Come for me." Darak had stood, grasping her tightly in his arms as she shuddered and clenched. The main crisis had passed, but her body still rocked with echoes of the pleasure he'd given her.

It was like some kind of tripwire had been cut. Little

explosions continued in her body long after his sinful kiss had ended.

"What's happening to me?" She clung to him, resting her head in the hollow of his neck.

"You're more than I ever imagined, Jana." His words sounded like praise. "I've heard of this reaction, but never seen it before."

Her body wouldn't stop quaking. She needed something more. Something only Darak could give. She just knew it.

"Help me, Darak," she whispered. She was afraid that, if he left her now, she would never recover from the loss.

"Do you trust me, Jana?" He seemed so earnest. "Do you trust me not to hurt you?"

That didn't even require thought. "I trust you, Darak. Only you."

"Thank the stars," he muttered, moving one hand between them. She didn't know what he was doing. She didn't care. Her body needed something to find relief, and he seemed to know what it was. She'd trust him to take care of her as he had since the moment she'd been separated from the collective. He'd been there for her, then. He'd take care of her now. She trusted him.

A moment later, she felt the invasion of what had to be his cock into her core. Shocked, she gasped. He was going to rape her. Just like the others. Damn him.

Her mind said those things, but her body was singing a different tune, she realized after a moment. Darak's possession wasn't the hard, uncaring thrust of a man who only sought his own satisfaction. No, Darak's cock claimed her slowly, with infinite care and patience. And it was a claiming. Not a conquering. The distinction was subtle, but she felt it in her soul.

"You're so tight, Jana. Are you all right?"

Tears formed in her eyes. No man had ever cared for her comfort. Not like Darak.

And her body welcomed him. Even as he pushed fractionally deeper, her body gushed in welcome of his possession.

"Jana, sweetheart. Tell me if I'm hurting you." He sounded so desperate she was compelled to answer.

"I'm okay," she whispered.

He thrust deep within her channel, stopping only when he was fully encased in her straining body. The quaking had grown worse with his claiming, though she felt better with him inside her than she had before.

"Believe me, sweetheart." He took a moment to comfort her as he rested within her. "I didn't mean for this to happen. Not this soon."

She believed him. It might be against her better judgment, but she believed he hadn't meant to fuck her so soon. Not that he'd ever made a secret of the fact that he wanted to fuck her. He was a rogue, but he was an honest one.

At the moment, she didn't really care. She just wanted the quaking to stop. She wanted to reach the fulfillment it promised and know finally what sex was all about. She'd never understood the big deal people made of it. Not until Darak.

He'd been her teacher in many things since she was cut off from the collective. He'd be her teacher in this. Heaven knew, there were few men better qualified.

"Are you ready, Jana?" he whispered near her ear. The next thing she knew, her earlobe was in his mouth and little shooting sensations of pleasure were transmitting from her earlobe to her clit, setting off another little chain of explosions inside her body.

"Please, Darak!" She couldn't take much more. Her every nerve ending was on fire with need. Need for something only Darak could give her. And she needed it now.

He began to move within her tight sheath, stroking in and stroking out in a slow rhythm that drove her wild. His cock was nothing like his finger had been. Or his tongue. This was as it was meant to be. His cock felt right inside her. Like it was made to be part of her. The girth and length of him was a perfect fit, the slight curve hitting that hidden spot over and over as he advanced and retreated.

Within moments, she was panting, gasping for air as his pace increased. She clutched his shoulders, keening and moaning as she reached for a completion only just out of reach. Her fingernails scratched his back lightly, encouraging him to move faster still. She was wild with need, and then, suddenly, the tidal wave of ecstasy broke over her, drowning the need in the most incredible satisfaction.

She floated in the seemingly endless sea of pleasure while Darak went rigid in her arms. She felt the warm flow of his seed inside her as he strained for the completion she gave him. It made her feel even better to know that she'd given him this same euphoric feeling. This completion that answered the question she'd had for so long about why people engaged in sex.

She finally understood. She knew now why so many people became fools for this kind of interaction. She understood why people would risk everything to be with someone they cared for.

Darak had taken such good care of her for so long. He'd helped her heal, and maybe, he felt an obligation toward her for that reason, but he'd also stuck around long after the initial healing had been complete.

At first, he'd annoyed her. He'd rubbed her the wrong way in every sense. But over time, she'd come to like his roguish ways and enjoy the teasing light in his handsome eyes. She'd come to care for him and anticipate the time they spent together.

Now, she knew what he was like as a lover. She wasn't sure how to feel about it. At the moment, she didn't want to think at all. She just wanted to float on the happy cloud of pleasure he'd introduced her to. Thinking could wait.

CHAPTER FIVE

Jana drifted in a state of utter, replete bliss. She felt motion, but it didn't really register until her head spun. Short seconds later, she felt a mattress against her back. Darak must have carried her into the bedroom and laid her down on the bed. At some point, he had disengaged their bodies, but her mind was hazy on the details. It wasn't possible to concentrate for long with the pleasant buzz of energy zinging through her veins.

"Are you all right?" Darak hadn't gone far. He lay beside her. His voice comforted her, though she felt so good—in no real need of comfort at the moment.

"Better than all right." She turned her head to meet his gaze, catching the concern shift to amusement.

"That good, eh?" It seemed like he couldn't resist teasing her, though he sobered quickly enough. One of his hands held hers, their fingers interlaced. He brought her knuckles to his mouth, to trace fine kisses on her skin. "I didn't mean for this to happen today, Jana."

"Lucky for you, I'm in a forgiving mood." She gave him a smile, surprised by how easy it was to bring a look of happiness to his face. She wasn't used to seeing happiness. Not since she'd been taken from her home as a young teen. The last happiness she remembered was that last, magical day on her family's horse farm. That perfect day before they came and stole her away.

"What makes you frown so, sweet Jana?" Gentle kisses on her hand brought her attention back to the man lying beside her.

How had she ended up here? She'd never intended to have sex again. Yet, here she was in bed with the worst rogue she'd ever met.

"Memories best forgotten."

"I hope not recent memories." He turned toward her, catching her eyes with a rueful expression.

"Memories of home," she found herself admitting. She hadn't meant to open up even that much. Must be that her sessions with the mind healer had gotten her used to talking more about things than she should. "Forget it. It's over, and I'm here now. I must deal with the present, not dwell on the past. Or so they say."

"They—whoever they are—are usually right. I've discovered that old adages usually hold some grain of truth within. I suppose that's how they become adages." He reached over to caress her cheek, and she found herself wanting to move into his touch.

That way lay danger. She had already let him go too far. It might be trying to close the stable door after the horses had escaped, but she had to do her best to guard her heart against his charm. She'd given him her body—all too easily, to her mind—but her heart would never be risked again.

Long ago, when she had first come under the collective's control, before her mind had been subjugated to their will, she had felt the heartbreak of losing those she loved. She remembered those feelings. They were the first to confront her when her mind was finally free. The death of her family may have happened years ago, but it was still fresh in her mind, and in her heart.

Having her little sister back in her life after all these years was a miracle. She loved Jeri more than anything in the universe, and she would not give her up again. No matter what. She would die before she let her heart be broken that way a second time.

Fear of that very thing filled her when she allowed herself to think about it. It was one of the many things she was working on with the mind healer.

Loving Jeri was enough. No way would Jana allow her heart to let anyone else inside its walled off boundaries. Not even the rogue who had so easily conquered her body.

Sex was one thing. Allowing herself to feel affection for him was entirely another.

But she liked him. Even though he annoyed her most of the time, there was something she liked about being around him. He was fun. He didn't take life too seriously, and he smiled a lot. Smiling was something she hadn't done much of in recent years. Not until Jeri and Micah had shattered the blue stone that had tied her mind to the collective. Not until her first waking moment of freedom, when she'd seen Darak's dark eyes hovering nearby, concern on his all-too-handsome face.

Then, she'd seen Jeri. Dear, sweet, Jeri. A little older now, but still the darling little sister she had played with as a child and loved so much. That vision had made her mouth move upward in the first genuine smile she had formed in years.

Tears had followed, but the smiles were plentiful from that moment forth. And Darak had been the cause of many of them. He seemed to take it as a personal mission to make her laugh, no matter how hard she resisted him.

And now, he'd been inside her. She wondered if the past moments of uninhibited passion would change the way he treated her now. Would he be more attentive? Or would he be done with her now that he'd gotten what he wanted?

She didn't think he was that mercenary, but then, what did she really know of his character? Most of the time, he played the court jester, hiding his real feelings behind a mask of humor. She doubted she'd ever seen the real Darak. Not for long at any rate.

She might have walls around her heart, but he had cast

iron gates around his to which only his family seemed to have the key. She'd seen him with them and thought perhaps he was more open with them than at any other time. Still, he guarded his true self almost as well as she tried to do.

They had that much in common, at least.

"So thoughtful, Jana." He brushed a lock of her hair back from her forehead. "Please tell me I haven't scarred you for life." A flare of something that could have been panic entered his eyes, but she dismissed it. She had to be reading things into his reaction that weren't really there. He cared for her on some level, but she doubted he truly cared enough to panic at the mere thought that she might now be regretting their actions.

"No scars from what we just did." She thought about that. "It's rather surprising, actually," she admitted. "Perhaps I was making too much of the idea of having sex again in my mind. The more I thought about it, the bigger the problem became."

"That is often the case when something is troubling me," he agreed. His gaze continued to search hers as if looking for the truth. "Too much analysis can blow something out of all proportion. Still, you should probably talk with Master Toombs about this." He looked worried, and she realized she was frowning at him.

"You want me to tell him we had sex?" She was shocked by the idea.

"Of course." Darak seemed to think nothing of discussing this most private act with the mind healer.

Of course, it might come up in the next session, but that was between Jana and Master Toombs. It would not be easy for her to talk about. Not in specific terms. She might allude to it, but on Mithrak, few people ever openly discussed sex.

"Do you want me to tell him?" Darak squeezed her hand as if to offer comfort, but his casual words nearly scandalized her.

"Darak!" She sat up and clutched a pillow to her midsection, effectively covering the important parts of her body. "I do not discuss such things as freely as you do."

"Stars save us from Mithrakian morals." He sat up, too, seemingly unconcerned by his nakedness. "Jana, you have to talk to him about this. It wasn't meant to happen, and I'm afraid it was too soon for you. After what you've been through, this could have done more harm than good."

"After what I've been through?" She repeated his words, appalled that he might have more knowledge of her past than she wanted him to know. "What's that supposed to mean? Have you all been discussing me behind my back? Is my sex life common knowledge?" Her voice rose with each accusation.

"Jana..." By contrast, Darak's voice was deathly calm, low and serious. "I know about the rapes."

All the blood drained out of her face, and she hugged the pillow tight. Only recently, with Master Toombs' help, had she been able to call the so-called matings the Wizards had subjected her to by their rightful name. Rape.

It was an ugly word for an even uglier deed. But it had happened to her. More than once. And worse than the rape had been the silence. Being cut off from the collective she'd come to depend on by that time. Silence in her own mind so that she could concentrate even more fully on the horror being visited upon her helpless body.

Tears leaked out of her eyes against her wishes. She turned away, but Darak saw. Of course he saw. And, like the hero he tried to portray, he reached for her, his arms offering comfort, not confinement.

Her mind resisted, but her body allowed the contact. Her body basked in his warmth, her confused emotions cracking the façade of control and allowing the sweet release of tears, the exquisite pain somehow pleasurable in that it allowed her to fully feel...to express...to being the slow process of healing.

Darak held her while she sobbed.

Each tear that leaked out of her eyes felt like a hammer

blow to his heart. Darak had never comforted a woman who needed it more. He could feel Jana's confusion and pain. Her hatred—of the past, he hoped—and not of him.

He understood, as well as a man who'd grown up free of oppression could understand such things. He felt the connection between them grow as she sobbed against his chest, and he didn't regret a single moment of it. He felt vulnerable, and that normally would have sent him running for the hills, but with Jana, it felt right to allow himself to feel these things. She was trusting him with her vulnerability. The least he could do was return the favor.

He said nothing, crooning to her wordlessly as he stroked her hair and held her tight against him. She clung in a satisfying way, though he hated the sound of her tears. Hated it for the pain it represented, not for any other reason. By the same token, he was glad she could express herself. That the torrent had let loose finally.

He'd talked extensively with Master Toombs about her. Not in specific detail of what she'd told the mind healer, but in broad terms about the stages she would most likely go through in her recovery. Master Toombs had been concerned that she hadn't broken down before this. He'd warned Darak to tread carefully, but like the impatient fool he was, Darak had forged ahead, full steam. The situation had quickly spiraled out of his control. He'd taken her long before he'd planned.

There was no doubt in his mind that they would be together at some point. He'd looked forward to it with every fiber of his being. He'd dreamed of it every night since he'd first touched her soft skin. But he knew it was too soon. He'd pushed her too far and had left them no alternative. Her body had gone up in flames, the way he'd hoped she would, but when the crisis point came and would not recede, he knew he had no choice but to see it through to the end.

She was paying for it now with the tears that broke his heart. He only hoped he hadn't done too much damage. Somehow, he'd help her through this. Somehow, he'd heal her heart if it took everything in him to do it. He wasn't a patient man by nature, but he'd cultivate the fortitude of a stone if it meant he'd be able to help her.

Jana was quickly becoming the center of his world. He didn't know where it would lead. He only knew that she was more important to him than his own life. When and how that had happened, he had no idea. The thought should have frightened him, but somehow…it felt right. As it should be. Fated.

Though Darak had never believed in fate before.

She began to quiet, her sobs dying down to little catches in her breath as her tears dried up. She swiped at her cheeks with her fingers, but Darak stilled her motions, kissing damp cheeks and soaking up the remaining tears with his lips.

"Do you feel better now?"

A sniffle was his answer as she drew away to fumble on the night table for the tissue box. He let her go, thinking the way she blew her nose so daintily was kind of cute. Everything about her was appealing on some level, even the puffy redness of her eyes. For that condition meant she had begun to heal in some small way. If Master Toombs was correct, perhaps this was the breakthrough they'd been waiting for. Darak only regretted that he'd brought it about in such a way. He didn't want her to equate his lovemaking with the horrors of her past. He wanted only to bring her joy—not memories of pain.

"I'm sorry." She threw the used tissue into the small wastebasket against the wall. She seemed unwilling to meet his gaze, and he didn't like it.

"For what?" he asked cautiously.

"For crying all over you. I'm usually never such a watering pot." The heat of a blush stained her cheeks to match her eyes.

"You deserved to cry for what was done to you." His tone was as gentle and serious as he could be, coaxing her gaze to his. "And it is I who owe you the apology."

"Let's say we're even." She finally met his gaze, and he felt relief when he saw the stable, calm acceptance there. Even a hint of humor. This was a peek at the Jana of his dreams. The woman he knew she could be.

Darak hugged her again, loosely, placing a smacking kiss on her lips as she smiled.

"We'd better get ready. The Council still wants to see you, and now, we're running late."

He released her to look for his clothes while she straightened the shimmersilk creation he'd had made just for her.

"It was worth it," she murmured as she brushed her fingers over the fabric. He heard her words, and they warmed his heart. "Good thing shimmersilk is such a forgiving fabric."

She left him in the bedroom while she went into the bathroom to clean up. When she returned, he nearly gasped at how beautiful she looked in the dress. She was a gorgeous woman, but the dress he'd designed showed off the otherworldly crystals in her skin to perfection. She looked like some kind of creature out of legend. A polar pixie or magical moondancer come to life just for him.

And he was definitely enchanted.

* * *

They took Darak's private shuttle to the Council compound. Few words were spoken between them, but she could feel his solid, silent support. A pleasant warmth continued to tingle through her body, echoes of the amazing feelings he'd taught her. And it seemed now she could read his expressions better than she could before. She could see behind the bad boy image to the more sensitive soul hidden beneath.

Or maybe she was just fooling herself. She wasn't sure.

The Council compound was larger than she expected, and the Council Chambers themselves were daunting, to say the least. Thankfully, she would be questioned first by the much smaller contingent of Master Mages and those ranked above. They didn't intend to subject her to the entire Mage Council. Not yet. Those of higher rank would determine if she needed to be questioned by the Council as a whole.

So, instead of facing hundreds of Mages, she only faced about fifty or sixty Mage Masters and a few Viziers. Jeri and Micah would be there, as well, along with one older woman named Elenor, the only other living Sha.

Jana had asked her sister to let the questioning proceed as it would. She didn't want her little sister appearing to take her side against the Council's most powerful delegates. Even though she was a Sha, Jeri was still an outsider, regardless of her marriage into one of the oldest and most powerful families on this planet.

The politics of power seemed to come naturally to Jana, which was curious. She certainly hadn't learned that at home on Mithrak. She could only guess such lessons had been learned during her time spent under the control of the Wizard collective.

It was a startling realization, and one she hadn't shared with anyone, yet. She knew things about the collective. She just knew them, without having conscious memory of them. Like the way she knew Jeri should tread carefully in the political arena where Jana was concerned. That wasn't something a sixteen-year-old farm girl would have thought of. But the seasoned starship captain she had been in the collective probably would have known how to navigate such political waters.

She had led the armada against Liata, for heaven's sake. She didn't really remember doing it, only the terrible aftermath. It had been agony. And ecstasy. To be free of the collective whispering in her mind. Free, at last.

Darak ushered her silently into the Council hall. They were using the main chamber, which was round with individual, movable pods attached to the sloping floor. The stage was a small round circle in the center, and the seating pods lined the upwardly sloping floor. They could detach from their moorings to move down to the staging area—or anywhere else for that matter—should the need arise. This arrangement helped when members seated in various parts of the hall needed to take the floor to address the full assembly.

The large chamber was mostly empty today, with only the first few circles of seating pods filled, clustering around the center stage where Jana would stand under their scrutiny. She didn't look forward to the next hours, but she understood they were something she had to get through in order to continue reclaiming her life. Being separated from the collective had only been the first step on a much longer journey. It was a journey she feared she must make alone.

Her sister Jeri couldn't do it for her. Nor did Jana want her to. This was something Jana had to do on her own. The collective had stolen her will many years before. It would take time, energy, and a wisdom she didn't think she had achieved just yet, to reclaim her individuality.

Darak had been a constant presence since she'd awoken aboard the *Circe*. He continued to plague her throughout her convalescence. And if she let him, she thought he might just move right in and overwhelm her fledgling existence. She didn't want that.

It would be so easy to give in and let him rule her life. He might just do it, too. If she let him. All the signs were there. He was a dominant male. He liked being in charge—and if she were being honest, she'd admit he was pretty good at it. He had a good head on his shoulders, though she would never admit that to his face. Although she'd given in to his sexual advances, she wanted to maintain a certain amount of distance from him emotionally. It was her only protection, flimsy though it may be.

Darak escorted her right onto the stage where she would sit for as long as they wished, asking her questions and pondering her motivations. There was a single chair placed in the center of the stage. Darak scowled as he looked at it.

"I'll get another chair. You are allowed an advocate to sit at your side, if you wish."

She stayed him, touching his arm as he turned to summon another chair.

"No." He paused, eyeing her critically. "I will face them on my own."

"Are you certain?" His gaze spoke of support and concern. She was touched, but she refused to let it show.

Jana tried to take on the mantle of the starship captain she had once been. She didn't remember much about those days, but if she had been able to lead an armada of ships—even while under the control of the collective—she must have something inside herself that could be called upon…some inner strength the collective had used and exploited.

Jana's days of exploitation were over. She would die before she allowed herself to come under anyone's power again. Now, she had to find those qualities that had made her useful to the collective and use them on her own behalf. The line in the sand had been drawn here and now. Here and now was where she had to find the resilience within herself to meet the challenge and stand tall.

And she would do it on her own. She had leaned on Darak long enough. Her wounds were as healed as they were going to get. Her emotional scars, she would carry for the rest of her days. The time had come for her to reclaim her life, starting here. Starting now.

"I must do this alone, Darak. Though I thank you for your support." There. That sounded both serene and strong.

Darak looked at her oddly, but she didn't acknowledge his questioning gaze with anything other than a small squeeze of her fingers on his arm. He stood a moment longer, holding her gaze while the room settled around them. The Mage Masters were organizing their documents, and one of the technical staff was setting up recording bots. The moment they were switched on, nothing would go unrecorded in this chamber. The idea made her uncomfortable, but it was just one more reason she needed to find her own balance in this uncertain sea. She couldn't depend on Darak to guide her. Not in this.

"I will sit with Micah and Jeri." He indicated the pod they sat in, just to her right, with a slight motion of his eyes as she removed her hand from his arm. "If you need me, all you have to do is crook your finger, and I will be at your side. You do not have to face them alone."

"Actually, I do," she disagreed with him in a polite but firm tone, a soft smile on her face, hoping he would understand.

Darak took both her shoulders in his hands. Before she could object, he bent to place a gentle kiss on her forehead. It almost felt like a benediction, but she recognized it for what it was. It was his way of staking his claim and declaring his support for her to all the gathered Talents, without speaking a single word.

He let her go as quickly as he'd taken hold of her, then stepped briskly to her right, to the pod where her sister and her new husband already sat, watching. Jana watched him go and caught the little wave Jeri sent her way. Jana nodded at her sister, then at Micah, acknowledging their presence as she took her seat.

The rustling in the chamber died down until one pod detached itself from the wall and floated down to settle in front of her. In it was a Vizier she didn't know. She recognized his rank from the formal robes he wore in Council, but she didn't know anything else about him.

"I am Vizier Balous," he introduced himself, using voice amplification so everyone in the chamber could hear.

She noted the mic that floated near her head in an offhanded way. Little visual and sound bots floated around her as unobtrusively as such things could. Everything from this moment forward would be recorded from multiple angles for posterity.

"Greetings of the Vizier Council and on behalf of the Master Mages and our esteemed Shas," the man continued by way of formal introduction to the proceedings. "Thank you for submitting to our questioning today. It is rare for us to be able to talk to someone separated from such lofty heights of power in the Wizards Collective."

He paused, but not long enough for her to return the greeting. Instead, he started right in on the questions. He started by asking her to state her name and planet of birth. Simple stuff. Then, he moved on to the more painful moments in her memory. He asked her to recount the day she was taken from her parents and everything she could remember afterward. It wasn't much. The collective had started whispering in her mind almost immediately, and it wasn't long before her thoughts had been overridden by the will of the collective.

Balous asked her to describe how the collective worked. She didn't always have sufficient words to explain the way the collective had taken her over, but she tried the best she could to make them understand.

When she claimed not to remember much from the time she was taken to the time she was freed, Balous pushed her hard. He alluded to the brief moments when she was free of the collective's whispers in her mind so she could be used by the men who tried to breed her. There were moments during that line of questioning where she nearly broke, but Jana refused to let mere memories of the past hurt her. She'd worked long and hard with the mind healer on exactly that— and the new memories of pleasure that Darak had given her helped her overcome the trauma of the past.

She realized now that the violence that had been done to her had nothing to do with pleasure. Darak had shown her that. He'd helped her make that final connection only hours before. She could look on the repeated rapes now as something sick and twisted that had been done to her. Not something she had participated in. Not something she'd had any sort of control over whatsoever.

She wanted to see the men who'd hurt her pay for their crimes. She no longer feared them. She no longer loathed herself for what *they* had done. She had come a long way from the woman who'd been shattered along with the blue stone that had exploded in her hand. The intense questioning only brought home how to her how much progress she'd made in such a short time.

Much of it due to Darak. She looked over at him, sitting with her sister and Micah in the pod to her right as there was a pause in the questioning. He looked angry at the line of questioning and ready to do battle on her behalf. She smiled—just a tiny lift of her lips—and he went still for a moment, his fists gradually unclenching.

The moment out of time helped them both. He calmed, and his strength seemed to float across the yards that separated them, into her. The questioning had been going on for over two hours. They'd allowed her a pitcher of ice water and a glass to partake of as she wished, but aside from the occasional pauses while the questioner organized his notes, she was kept center stage, on constant alert. It was tiring, but Darak's silent support gave her renewed energy. She faced Balous' next questions with a clearer mind for having taken a moment to connect with her new lover.

Lover. Yes, that's what he was to her now. Her first lover. The only real lover she had ever known. The men who had come before were criminals, not lovers. No, that distinction was Darak's alone.

Balous let her sit quietly for a few minutes while he outlined the career of Commodore Jana Olafsdoter of the Wizards Collective. Apparently, the Council had an extensive file on her with all kinds of intelligence reports of her doings, complete with holographic recordings. There was even one of her being elevated to Commodore in a ceremony she barely remembered. Jana was fascinated by the footage and sat forward in her seat to study it as it was projected on the stage just in front of her for all to see.

"Do you recall this occasion?" Balous asked.

"Vaguely. I remember the uniform and the braid on the epaulets. My…yeoman…Marnie—that's her standing behind me and to the left—had a hard time getting the new decorations on straight. She cut her hand very badly, and I—"

"You what?" Balous prompted when she broke off midsentence.

The memory that came to mind was just too strange. Jana remembered something of her powers before being cut loose from the collective that didn't jive with anything she'd learned about herself since.

"I healed her." Jana shocked herself with the admission. "It was a misuse of the power granted to me by the collective, which is why I think I can remember it now. It was my will that she be spared the pain and disfiguration of her injury. It was the real me trying to do something for a friend." Jana was amazed by the revelation.

"Did you use the blue stone in your command staff to channel that ability?"

"No. It was something I could do by myself, without the stone." She looked downward at her hands, realizing she'd had the power within herself to heal her friend. Why hadn't she known she could heal? And why didn't the others here tell her? Surely, Darak—or somebody—had already figured out where her Talents lie.

"Is healing something you could do before you were taken by the collective? Your testimony to this point has indicated that you didn't have any true manifestation of your Talent before they came for you. Is that correct? Or do you wish to amend your testimony?"

"No need to amend. I didn't even realize until this moment that I was able to heal. I'm not sure if I still can. It was easy, then, but I had the power of the collective at my disposal, even when I wasn't in contact with the stone. I have no idea where my Talents lie at the present moment. I was told not to try using any power at all until I was healed from the blast."

"So, you have not been tested since leaving the collective?" Balous had the air of someone who already knew the answer to his own question, but she supposed he needed to get her to answer for the sake of everyone else.

"No, Vizier Balous. I have not been tested as to strength

of Talent or the directions in which it lies. I have only just remembered, with the aid of your hologram, that I even had a yeoman named Marnie, much less that, once upon a time, I was able to heal her hand."

"Do you feel well enough to engage in use of your Talent now? Have your doctors said anything to you about it?" Again, he shuffled through reports, and she'd bet he had full disclosure of her medical condition.

"They've counseled me to take it slow and easy. Frankly, I've been afraid to try anything with these..." She gestured to the crystals embedded in her skin. "Nobody seems to know what will happen when and if I try to use my Talent with these shards of the control crystal still in my body."

"Yet, you have shields," Balous prompted.

"Yes. Thanks to my sister, Jeri, and her husband Micah, and his cousin, Darak." She nodded over to the pod where all three sat together. "They've extended their shields to me while I healed and continue to do so."

"Do you consider yourself healed now?"

"For the most part. There are some things that will never be as they once were. Most notably the blue jewelry that now seems to be a permanent part of my attire." She got a chuckle out of that from a few members of the audience. As time went on, she became less afraid of Balous and his questions.

"I'm glad you brought that up. May we examine the crystals for the record?"

"How so?" She sat up straighter, wondering what they wanted to do to her now.

"Nothing to fear, milady. Simply some close-ups with the bots so that everyone can get a good view of the larger crystals. This is something none of us have ever seen before. We have the medical reports, but a visual record would be helpful, as well."

"All right," she agreed hesitantly as the little floating bots whirred closer. She tried to sit still, but couldn't help flinching when one of the little things came perilously close to her breast.

Another enterprising little bot began to shine different wavelengths of light at one of the larger stones, eliciting a rainbow of colors that shone throughout the chamber. Everyone was watching with intense interest as she allowed the examination.

From light, the bot progressed to sound, shooting beams of different wavelengths of sound waves at the crystals. The light hadn't elicited any sort of response, but the sound was starting to tickle, then singe, then burn as the tone increased in pitch. Jana shifted uncomfortably in her chair until the slight burning sensation escalated to outright pain.

Without thought, she moved her hand and swept the small bot away. She hadn't touched it, but it went flying across the chamber, anyway, narrowly missing one of the Vizier's heads on its way to smash against the wall. It fell to the floor, broken into several pieces.

Jana was shocked, as were some of the people watching, but others seemed coldly satisfied—as if they expected her to turn violent, and she had only just confirmed their suspicions. Others, she was surprised to see, looked pleased. And Darak, when she finally turned to look at him, wasn't hiding his anger very well.

She didn't think the anger was directed at her. Instead, if looks could kill, Vizier Balous would be nothing but a little pile of cinders at her feet.

"I'm sorry." She spoke into the silence. "I just reacted. I didn't mean to cause harm. It just—" She broke off, not liking to admit any weakness.

"What, *dama*? Why did you use your power in such a way?"

She hadn't really realized, until Balous spoke, that she'd used her power at all. But then, how could the bot have flown across the room to shatter against the wall? She hadn't touched it. No, she must have used her power, without realizing it.

"Again, I apologize for my lack of control. I've been counseled not to use my Talent until given leave to do so. I did not do it consciously. My only excuse is that it was instinct to react when the bot's actions began to get…uncomfortable." Even now, she didn't want to admit the bot's sound waves had been downright painful. She didn't want to give anyone ideas about weapons that could be used against her.

Strategy, it seemed, was second nature to her now, though the farm girl she had been wouldn't have hesitated admitting being hurt. Jana, the ship's captain and armada leader, knew better, though. She didn't trust these Councilors to not use any perceived weakness against her.

"Have you always had such pinpoint accuracy with your telekinesis?" Balous changed his line of questioning.

"I'm not sure. A lot about my abilities was clouded by the collective's voice in my mind. Most of my memories of actually using my Talent are fogged over by the presence of the collective. The few times my mind was free, I was usually subdued by a much stronger mind, physical restraints, or both. Usually both. I never had an opportunity to fight back using my Talent during those times. I was cut off from the collective only after I'd already submitted to being restrained."

It was an unpleasant truth and one that she tried to recite as unemotionally as possible. She tried not to look at the people all around her and their varying expressions of horror, grim resolve or pity. At least these people seemed to think what had been done to her was wrong. That was more than the collective believed. Indeed, they had designed the torture and facilitated it to further their own nefarious goals. The collective was evil, in that regard and many others. The Voice that ruled it was inhumane.

That was a truth Jana had come to accept as she lay recovering from her injuries. The mind healer had helped her see more of that truth. As had Darak and his family.

For all that she was still uncomfortable in the extreme with the sexual morals of the Talents of Geneth Mar, she respected the humanity and compassion of its people. They'd all been gentle with her as she'd been healing. They had helped her. Coddled her, even. That was something she had never had from the collective.

She had not had human kindness since she'd been abducted from her home and forced to serve the collective.

The questioning went on for a little while longer, but eventually, Balous seemed to run out of topics, and she began to feel very tired. Darak made a motion to adjourn, citing her obvious fatigue and the lateness of the hour, and the Councilors agreed.

She noted that they wanted her back the next day—and further reserved the right to call her back at any time for more questions—with a resigned sigh. It would take much for these people to trust her, and frankly, she didn't blame them. How could they know if she was trustworthy when she didn't even know her own heart?

CHAPTER SIX

The next day's questioning was much like the last until the final hours. Balous and another man, who had been introduced only as Specitar Kane, quizzed her about the collective. They wanted to know how it worked. How she perceived it in her mind. How the blue crystal that had been in her control staff and had subsequently blown up in her hands, worked—both before it had shattered, and now that parts of it were imbedded in her skin.

They asked probing questions, and when Balous left the podium for the final hour, allowing Kane to question her alone, they turned brutal. Kane, it seemed, was the real interrogator. He pounded his questions home like nails through her skull, each one more difficult to answer than the last.

He pushed her to her limits and beyond. His merciless questions made her want to lash out, and she felt her power gathering. Only Darak's worried look made her refrain and seek control.

Perhaps, that was Kane's task. To test her control.

Deciding that must be the case, she calmed by slow degrees, noting with one part of her mind, how good he was at his job. Remnants of the old, warrior Jana admired his skill.

And then, suddenly, he stopped. And smiled.

"It seems the test is at an end." He bowed his head, then turned toward the assembled Talents, who had all been watching closely. "She has divined the intent of my work here and further testing will not be productive. However, I can say that when pushed to a level I have seldom used on any other subject, she did not lash out. She sought control rather than violence. She has great mental discipline, which I did not expect."

Neither had Jana, if she was being honest. Untrained when the collective took her, she didn't think she really had any skills of her own, but maybe she'd been wrong. Maybe the control they had taught her as part of the collective was something that stayed with her, even now that she was cut off from them. Maybe it was instinctual. Something that, once learned, could not be unlearned.

"Then, it is time," Balous said, returning to the podium. "It is with some reluctance that we have reached consensus on this matter, Master Darak." Darak rose and came over to stand near her as Balous addressed him directly. "We need you and the *Circe* out there, being our eyes and ears, but we have registered your desire not to be parted from Jana Olafsdotter. While we would rather she be tested further, we also recognize the threat she could pose to our planet and people. Perhaps, as you have argued, the safest place for her, at the moment, is in the vastness of space. I fear she may yet pose a danger to you and your crew, but if it is your wish—and if your crew still agrees—then we grant leave for you to depart, with Jana Olafsdotter, as soon as you are ready."

Jana tried her best not to show her surprise and alarm. Darak was leaving and he wanted her on the ship with him? This was all news to her.

More troubling was the Council's belief that she could be a danger. Jana knew they were probably right, but it still hurt to have them say it out loud like that. She didn't want to harm anyone on Geneth Mar. Not anymore. She still didn't agree with their morals, but she had come to realize they were still just people—raised with different expectations of behavior than she had been—but basically good for all their differences. She didn't want to see them or their planet come to harm. Especially not because of her.

But she didn't want to leave Jeri. While it was true that Jeri was busy with her new life and husband, Jana craved any bit of attention her little sister could spare. They'd been parted for so long. Jana had only just rediscovered her family, and now, she was being asked—no, *told*—to leave her again. Jana didn't like it.

And she especially didn't like the highhanded way Darak had ordered her life. He'd requested her presence on his ship. He'd petitioned the Council. All this had been done without her knowledge or consent. It was almost as bad as being ordered around by the Voice of the collective. Only now, she was awake and aware of being manipulated. Which made it somehow worse.

"Specitar Agnor will be tasked with testing her further," Balous continued even as Jana's mind spun at what she was hearing. "He will also be asked to do what training is necessary to make her safer to be around, as will you, Master Darak, as your other duties allow. She is to be observed, and reports filed on her progress any time you have a secure connection. Under no circumstances is she to be allowed to interfere in the ship's duties or its crew. How you achieve this is up to your discretion." Balous's gaze moved from Darak back to Jana, and she felt the weight of his regard. "Now, *dama*, please try to make the best of this. I know it is not necessarily your will to go on this journey, but we have our reasons for sending you. All of those stated and one other I will put forward, hoping to ease your mind…"

Balous shocked her by coming over to her and taking her hand in his. She felt the vibrations of his sincerity as their resting power met and tingled against each other.

"The gift of foresight is rare, but it does exist. Please believe me when I say that I have foreseen that you must be on the *Circe* at this time. I don't know what will happen, but I do know it is where you are meant to be. Take what comfort you can from this foreknowledge, if indeed, you can take any."

He released her hand and walked back to his position behind the podium. Jana was familiar with foresight, though the collective had none. Something about the merging of minds and Talents dampened any such gifts that might have occurred in the population. The Voice scoffed at such things. It had said that the only destiny is the one it forged itself. It paid no heed to prophecy or visions, and the collective followed suit.

Jana didn't know what to make of Balous's words. He was a powerful being if he was part of this gathering. The others in the room did not bat an eye at his pronouncement. Apparently, they all believed in his ability to foresee parts of the future. While she wouldn't put too much stock in such things, she understood at least part of his motivation for deciding her fate in such a cavalier manner. He truly believed she needed to be on that ship, out of harm's way for the people and planet of Geneth Mar.

Well, if that's how they felt, so be it. Jana would not stay where she was not wanted. She felt a pang of loss for having to part from Jeri, but now that they'd been reunited, Jana held hope that they would be able to comm each other and perhaps see each other in person from time to time. Those stolen moments would have to do. The Council was giving her precious little choice in the matter.

As the Council meeting ended, Jana stood and found she could not look at Darak. Her eyes were downcast as she contemplated all that had happened that day. Drained by the questioning, the pronouncements and the emotional upheaval in general, she walked off the stage toward her sister.

Jeri met her and caught her in a big hug that made Jana feel marginally better. Of course, it also made her sad, realizing she would not be here to receive such hugs in the very near future. No, they were making her leave her only living relative behind, and it caused a deep sadness.

"Don't worry, Jana," Jeri whispered near her ear. "It'll all work out. I'll miss you, but you have a destiny to chase." Jeri drew back and met Jana's gaze. "There are things you must do that cannot be accomplished here. Fears you must face. Questions you must answer. Things you have to reconcile before you can truly be at peace in your own skin."

"Are you a foreseer, too, now?" Jana felt the need to tease, even as her heart broke.

Jeri chuckled and let her go. "No, but even I can see that you need time—and space—to heal. You're not a planet-bound sort of woman. Even as a girl, you always dreamed of the stars. I think you belong out there, among them. That's where your true self lies, and it would be selfish of me to keep you here, when you so plainly need to be out there, finding your destiny."

"With Darak?" Jana shot a look of disgust toward the man who was talking with Balous some feet away.

"Maybe. Who knows? But I do know he is a good man and an excellent teacher. He will guide you without smothering you. Despite all his antics and his irreverent sense of humor, he's a good soul. He will help you, as he has since the moment you fell away from the collective. He feels responsible for you, and that's not such a bad thing, once you realize he's got both immense power and an enormous ability for compassion."

"An immense ego, you mean," Jana chided, but only half-heartedly.

"That, too," Jeri agreed, laughing as they walked toward the exit where Micah waited. "Don't worry, though. You couldn't ask for a better man to fight alongside when things get tough. Don't discount his abilities. His ego may be large, but so is his Talent and ability to think creatively in the midst of battle."

"If you say so." Jana decided to let the matter rest as they left the Council Chamber. "I just dread being stuck on a ship with him. He's going to drive me crazy. You know that, right?"

Jeri laughed, as did Micah, who had heard the tail end of

their conversation. Darak joined them a moment later as they all made their way back to the family home for a final meal together. Jana knew the *Circe* was scheduled to leave tomorrow. It had been the talk of the house for the past few days. Little had she realized, she'd be flying away with her when she left.

* * *

It was hard to leave, but when the time came, Jana tried to keep her chin up. Darak was surprisingly sympathetic and didn't chide her about her silent acceptance of her fate. Instead, he gave her room to deal with her new situation, which she appreciated.

She hadn't been on the *Circe* in a while, but she remembered the smell of the ship. Clean, crisp, albeit recycled, air the likes of which one did not usually find on a starship. Those who maintained the *Circe's* systems did a much better job than most, and the systems themselves were top of the line. There were no half-measures on this ship. No expense had been spared in building her—or in her recent refit.

Jana had first seen the *Circe* as an enemy, blocking her armada's conquest of a peaceful agrarian world. She remembered bits and pieces of that confrontation only because seeing her sister again, after so many years had passed, had jarred Jana from the collective's hold. It hadn't been for long, but long enough for Jana to have some clear recollections of the first moments she'd seen Jeri again and the horror she had felt at the situation in which she had found herself.

Jana had been appalled to realize she'd been trying to kill her only living relative. Her beloved little sister. The sister she had thought lost long ago, only to find her alive and well. And on this ship, the *Circe*. While Jana had commanded a fleet intent on death and destruction. Intent on blasting the *Circe* from the sky above that little blue planet with the strange sun and the blue-skinned people who lived there.

The collective had reined her in, trying to subdue her mind. The blue crystal in her staff of power had glowed fiercely and burned its power along the pathways in her mind as the Voice of the collective had screamed for her attention, demanding her obedience.

But, at the last, Jana liked to believe that she had overcome the Voice. At least a little. She'd taken a stand against it—even if only in her mind—to help save her sister's life.

They hadn't really discussed it, and that was the one thing all the questions had never asked. The Councilors just seemed to assume that Jana had been both deaf and blind—as she had often been as a subject of the collective—and had not been able to help in those final moments. But Jana thought she knew differently. And she hoped Jeri did, too. Maybe, someday, they'd be able to talk about it, but for now, the scars were still too fresh.

Jana thought maybe she needed to discover who she really was first, before she delved into who she had been.

When she had awoken aboard the *Circe* the first time, in a heavily shielded suite, the annoying Darak at her bedside, Jana had been scared. She had tried hard not to let it show, but she thought maybe Darak had sensed her fear. She'd been cut off from the collective for the first time in years, and while it was a relief to have control over her own actions once more, there was also near-paralyzing fear for what would come next.

Then, Darak had smiled at her. And her midsection had made the strangest little internal flip. Something stirred to life, and no matter how much she fought against it, Jana had found herself attracted to a man for the first time since being abducted as a young girl.

But this attraction wasn't like the schoolgirl crushes she'd had when she was little. No, this was something that made her blood bubble with fire and her stomach clench with unknown desires.

And all that for a man who had whored around the galaxy, bedding everything with a pussy for all of his adult life. The very idea made her sniff with disdain. How could she be attracted to such a rogue? A Council gigolo. A gorgeous specimen of manhood who made her want dark, dangerous, scandalous things.

The bastard.

She had been weak, but she had turned her head away from him. She hadn't wanted him to see and possibly read her damning desires in her eyes. She'd expected him to act with disdain toward her. Or perhaps rudeness. Even force. But he'd done none of those things. He'd shown her only kindness and caring. Healing touches and warmth when, for the past years, under the collective's power, she'd had none.

He'd made her tremble. She could have so easily become dependent on him. He'd healed her. He'd asked for nothing in return. He'd treated her with kindness and teasing innuendo. He'd even kissed her, but he'd never pressed his advantage, even when she was so damaged she couldn't have fought off a horsefly.

Even while she'd healed on the planet, he'd been keeping track of her progress, visiting often. Charming every female he passed as a matter of course. She'd watched him deal out fond kisses on old, withered cheeks and bring a bloom of color to those cheeks with his devastating smile and charming words. He always had a kind word for the older women and a teasing wink for young and old alike.

It seemed no female was immune to his charm. Jana had tried so hard to be the exception, but it all seemed for naught. Not that she'd let him know the extent of her uncontrollable attraction for him. She would die of embarrassment if he ever found out how she really felt about him.

And now, they were stuck together on this small ship where the crew engaged in sexual orgies whenever the mood struck. Jana didn't know how she was going to handle this. Already, she knew she could not hide out in the shielded room she'd been in before.

She'd been assigned duties on the ship, to help keep it running. She was on a work rotation with everyone else. She'd been given crew quarters. It was a luxurious room for a starship, but its placement was problematic. Her room was directly next to the captain's quarters—Darak's suite. In order to get out of the crew area of the ship, she had to use a corridor that passed not only his door, but also the open hatchway to the recreation area.

Jana knew that was where off-duty crew hung out together—and engaged in all sorts of scandalous activities. She tried not to look as she walked past the open arch of the room, but she had already seen two of the younger crewmembers fucking the blue-skinned Loadmaster—a woman named Trini. One had been seated on the huge couch while Trini rode his cock, and then, as Jana watched helplessly, the other young man had stuck his cock in her rear. Trini's moans followed Jana down the hall, much to her mortification.

When she finally arrived on the bridge for her turn on comm duty, she knew her face was bright red. Her cheeks were hot, but there was nothing she could do about it except to take her station and pretend nothing was amiss. It wasn't until Darak walked onto the bridge a moment later and caught her eye that she knew her ruse wasn't quite working. He gave her a knowing smile before turning to receive the reports from the previous shift.

It was a small ship, tightly run, with a small crew. Jana had met most of them already, and found it easier than she had thought it would be to make a place for herself among them. At least as far as ship's duties went. A lot of the skills she must have learned while under control of the collective were coming back to her. Skills related to reading navigational charts, assessing system readouts, plotting courses in three-dimensional space while allowing for fluctuations due to gravity wells and debris fields. All of these specialized space faring skills had stayed with her, much to her surprise.

A lot of what she had been subject to since her

kidnapping, all those years ago, was a blur. Frankly, she was glad of that. The little she did remember of the things that had been done to her was horrific enough. The mind healer had told her that some of it might never come back, and maybe that was a blessing. He told her that the human mind often developed surprising ways to protect itself, and that perhaps, her mind had done so.

They'd managed to retrieve the memories that had been sitting closest to the surface. Truly awful things that she had to deal with in order to recover and move on with her life. But some parts of her experience were more deeply buried, and best left the way, at least for the time being. He'd warned her that being on a ship in space again might trigger certain recollections—and it certainly seemed that way, judging by the skill set she had managed to access. Maybe more would come back to her. Or maybe not.

Patience was the order of the day, though Jana couldn't quite remember if she had ever been a patient person. Regardless, these things couldn't be rushed, she had been warned. If the memories came, she would have to deal with them as best she could.

Jana found work on the bridge to be both interesting and stimulating, though a small part of her itched for command. The captain's chair looked awfully comfortable, and somehow, she seemed to recall having felt right at home in command of an armada.

When such thoughts occurred to her, Jana felt distinctly uncomfortable. She'd heard what she had done with that armada. They'd been following her commands—her lead— when she had ordered the destruction of a good portion of the peaceful, agricultural planet of Liata. Many innocent people had died, and it had been by her command.

The only way she could deal with the guilt was that she knew those commands had come from the Voice. The collective had spoken to her through the command crystal. The Voice had been her constant companion. She had been its pawn, its dupe, its puppet. She hadn't really been in control of the armada. Hells, she hadn't even been in control of her own mind. She had simply fulfilled the Voice's commands, issuing orders to the armada that had been implanted into her consciousness. So, it hadn't really been her decision to kill all those people. It had been the Voice. The hateful, insidious, despicable Voice.

The Voice of the collective had controlled her utterly and made her do things she couldn't even bring herself to contemplate. It had ruined her life. It had taken away all of her choices, all of her hope, and what she thought would be all of her life.

And then, Jeri had come. Jeri and this tiny, formidable, spunky little ship full of adventurers and Talents. The *Circe* and her crew had saved Jana. Unexpected, unprecedented and unanticipated, this ship had brought salvation, though at the time, Jana hadn't been able to appreciate it with the Voice still whispering in her mind and controlling her thoughts.

And it had brought Darak.

But the Council was the sworn enemy of the collective. So many of Jana's missions had been against Council worlds and holdings. She knew they viewed her as an enemy, and her actions as acts of war against the Council. She had fully expected to be put on trial for war crimes when they arrived, but instead, she had been taken to hospital and healed.

Her body would never be the same, though they'd tried their best to help her. Mentally, they had tried to help her, too. The mindhealer had done all he could with her in the time they had together, but had told her honestly the full healing would take a lot more time. He had helped her begin the process, but it was an ongoing one, that could last the rest of her life.

Being busy helped. She liked the routine of the ship. She had a job and a purpose in helping keep the ship functioning at top levels. She enjoyed sitting watch on the bridge with the others and had become friendly with some of the crewmembers, to a certain extent. There was still a degree of distrust. They didn't really know what to make of her. They all knew of her origins. They'd seen her lead the attack force against Liata.

And they'd seen her after. When she was too damaged to move and close to death. And since most of this crew had been on that voyage, they had all been affected by the shattering of the crystal.

Most of them probably should have stayed on Geneth Mar, continuing to learn about their new abilities and levels of power, but everyone from the old crew—with the exception of the former captain of the *Circe* and his new bride—had signed on for Darak's maiden voyage as captain and newly minted StarLord. Agnor, in particular, probably should have stayed behind. His increase in power was still not fully understood. He'd started the previous voyage as a Specitar, and while he remained one, he was able to do so much more than he could have previously.

Specitars usually fit somewhere between Mages and Mage Masters in overall strength, but excelled only in specialized areas. Agnor's specialty was telepathy. Even before the change, he could reach farther with his mind than almost anyone, except perhaps Shas and most Viziers, but his other psychic skills were not that strong, except perhaps his cognition. He had developed his mental processes— influenced by the telepathy—so that he could solve scientific problems faster than most computers, using human intuition that comps just didn't have.

Jana had learned that Specitars were given seats on the Mage Council but also had their own Board of Specitars, which was a subsection of the Council devoted to scientific and technological matters. Agnor also served a special function aboard the *Circe*. He was there to send telepathic messages directly back to Geneth Mar. There was no known way to intercept such messages, which made them utterly secure.

But distance was still a factor. At least it had been on that last voyage. After the psi wave, Agnor's telepathic reach had extended far beyond anything anyone had seen before. He'd been able to 'path directly back to their home planet from half a galaxy away, without using the relay Talents employed and stationed around the galaxy by Geneth Mar's intelligence service. Agnor had 'pathed directly to the Grand Vizier, Darak's Uncle Brandon, right after the change, and it had raised many eyebrows.

Agnor should still probably be back on Geneth Mar, being tested and examined. His was a rare Talent, among so many Talented people. Just as Micah and Jeri were now cosseted Shas, Agnor, too, should probably be receiving similar treatment, but he had steadfastly refused to give up his position as science officer and comm tech on the *Circe*. Underneath the ascetic exterior and formal robes of the Specitar, Agnor seemed to have an adventurer's heart.

And he was as horny as the rest of these Council folk. More than once, Jana had seen him balls deep in one of the female crewmembers. He hid a very lean, muscular body under those robes, and Jana was embarrassed to admit she had taken notice. She explained away her fascination with watching him fuck Seta in the rec room as the shock of realizing the tall man was hiding quite a physique under those concealing robes of his. And, if her ladyparts seemed to twinge in…yearning? That couldn't be possible. Could it?

Jana had turned away from that particular scene, both confused and embarrassed. She'd gone to her cabin and tried in vain to sleep for what seemed like hours. When she finally emerged from her room the following shift, she was tired and out of sorts. Darak left her alone, for once, not commenting on her mental state—which she was certain he knew. He was still shielding her when she wasn't in her cabin, and he had to pick up on her frazzled energy.

The cabin was the only place of true privacy for her. She was able to engage a reflective field, which would not allow anyone to use psi energy without a great deal of pain. She was safe within the field. Safe from the murmuring voices of the collective. Safe from the empathic senses of the rest of the crew—particularly Darak. Just…safe.

But it really was all just an illusion. She was in a small ship, hurtling through space, possibly headed into danger. The future was uncertain. They were on a Council mission, and that could mean just about anything. Jana hadn't been told the specifics of Darak's orders. She didn't need to know them. All she had to do was play her part, as requested, when the time came.

She didn't know what that would entail exactly, but she had agreed to help the Council and aid Darak in his mission. She had switched allegiances. Not that she'd ever had a choice in her allegiance to the collective. They'd simply demanded. At least the Council had asked nicely.

Jana wasn't quite sure what they would have said, or done, it she had refused. For her sister's sake, and for her own, she really had no other choice than to become a good little citizen of the Council. Jana had nowhere else to turn. The only family she had left in the entire universe was her sister. So, where Jeri went, Jana would follow. They'd been separated long enough as it was.

* * *

Frustration wasn't something that Darak handled well. In fact, he couldn't remember a time in his life where he'd been under more pressure and unable to accomplish what he'd set out to do. In this case, all he really wanted was to help Jana recover fully. And, for a citizen of a Council world, full recovery included sex. Lots and lots of sex.

But Darak had to tread lightly with Jana. She'd been through things that the vast majority of people on Council worlds never experienced. With the level of Talent all around on every Council world, the empaths and telepaths, sensitives and telekinetics, rapists never got very far in their plans before somebody became aware and did something about it.

Jana's case was unique in Darak's experience. He knew how to heal her physical wounds, but the mental ones made him feel just a bit out of his depth. He'd spent a lot of time with the mind healer, asking questions and trying to learn as much as he could before they left Geneth Mar, but it didn't feel like enough. He'd been counseled to watch and wait for Jana to make the first move. She had to be Darak's guide. She had to decide when she was ready to take the next steps of her road to full recovery.

So, when he'd come upon her watching Agnor fuck Seta senseless in the rec room one evening, he'd held back in the corridor and watched her reaction. She hadn't run away. Not at first. No, Darak had been surprised to note that Jana had stayed in the doorway, watching the oblivious couple for a few very long minutes.

The expression on her face had been hard to decipher. Darak had viewed her from the side, stationed farther down the hall where she couldn't see him, so he could see her profile. Her eyes had widened, and her mouth opened in shock, but before too long, curiosity had replaced surprise, though her cheeks had flamed with heat. She was embarrassed by what she saw, but also intrigued.

Darak took that as a hopeful sign—until she'd fled.

He gave a great deal of thought to how he should handle her. She seemed tired and cranky. He didn't want to push her so off balance that she lashed out. He didn't want her hatred. Far from it. So, he decided to let any teasing he otherwise would have engaged in with any other crewmember, pass without comment. Something was building—changing—within her, and he didn't want to stifle it in any way. If she was finally ready to come out of her shell, he wanted to do all he could to encourage it.

Which is why, the very next day, he arranged something that might just push her to the next level.

CHAPTER SEVEN

Darak had taken great care in organizing the crew schedule, with the full endorsement and cooperation of the bridge crew. In particular, he arranged a nice long double shift for Sita, to get her into the nighttime rotation, so she could keep a better eye on the yeoman crewmembers that were running the graveyard shift. It was something they had intended to do all along, but hadn't quite gotten there, yet. Now was as good a time as any and had the added benefit of creating a scenario that might be beneficial to Jana's recovery.

Or not. Darak didn't know how this was going to turn out. He might just be pushing too hard.

But one thing was for certain—he couldn't go on with this incredible level of frustration eating at him. He had to try something. It would either work or fail miserably, but at least they'd be moving in a direction—forward or back, he just wasn't sure.

Seta sat her double shift, making a great show of yawning and stretching as Darak and Jana stepped onto the bridge, ready to start their own daytime shift. Day and night were merely conveniences used to help the crew keep track of time, but the terms were ambiguous when you were on a spaceship, jogging from star to star.

"Good morrow, Seta, how goes the night shift?" Darak

asked, unable to conceal his good mood. He was eager to see how the events he had put into motion would play out.

"I guess I'm not as young as I used to be, Captain," Seta said with a good-natured smile. She had once been a sex slave and came from a highly permissive world where some Talents trained to bring others to orgasm using their powers of telepathy or telekinesis alone.

Seta dressed in skimpy clothing, which emphasized her lovely body. More often than not, her breasts were visible, the piercings in her nipples adorned with a variety of jewelry she had picked up or been given by past lovers and friends. She was a highly sexual being, and every man on the crew had enjoyed her warmth and open nature many times, including Darak, though come to think of it, he hadn't had sex with her—or any woman, for that matter—since they'd rescued Jana.

Darak knew that was significant, but he didn't spend too much time thinking about it. His focus had to be on Jana and her recovery. Whatever they would be to each other would sort itself out later. If she could get past her scars and the horrible things that had been done to her under the collective's despotic rule.

"I'm sorry to hear that, Seta. Perhaps Agnor could give you a boost before you leave, if you're so inclined." Darak nodded to the tall science officer who had just arrived on the bridge for his shift.

Agnor smiled at Seta, and she smiled back at him. They were about to enact the plan Darak had hatched with them hours ago.

"Would you care to join us?" Seta asked Darak with a purring sort of smile as she stepped into Agnor's arms.

Darak was aware of Jana's quick intake of air as if she'd been startled by the question. He was pleased by her reaction. She was aware of what was about to happen, and somehow, his participation—or lack of it—mattered to her.

"Sadly, no. Not this time. Someone has to run the ship, after all," Darak quipped. Seta laughed as Agnor swooped down and placed a kiss on her neck.

Then, Seta did something that wasn't in the plan. She looked pointedly at Jana, making eye contact as Agnor ravished her neck and moved lower.

"Darak hasn't been with any of us since becoming captain. Even before that," Seta told Jana in a conversational tone, even as Agnor began to kiss her nipples. "I'm not sure what you did to him, Lady Jana, but I think you might've ruined him for any other woman." Seta smiled and winked at Jana. "Lucky girl."

Seta moaned as her head dropped back, and she wrestled Agnor's robes open, reclining back on the nav board she had switched into standby mode when her shift ended. It was just the right height, Darak knew from prior experience. And Agnor didn't waste any time, sliding deep into Seta's receptive body.

Jana's face was scarlet as she stood frozen, not too far from Darak. He was afraid she would run, but instead, she seemed rooted to the spot, fascinated by what she was witnessing. Good. Darak could work with that.

He walked silently over to her, sliding his arms around her waist from behind.

"Do you like what you see?" he whispered against her ear. He felt her shiver in his arms, and he couldn't help but smile.

"Are they going to...? Right there?" Jana wondered, still staring and seeming scandalized.

"Why, yes, I believe they are. I know for a fact that console was made with this sort of activity in mind. When we designed the ship, we built it for comfort."

Jana sputtered a bit, then finally turned slightly in his arms to look at him. "You designed a ship for fornicating?"

Yeah, she was definitely scandalized. And outraged, too, if he didn't miss his guess.

It was adorable.

"Well, she served other purposes, too. We fitted the *Circe* with the most advanced systems available in every respect, but I will admit freely that the happiness of the crew was high on the list of priorities. And we Council Talents do like our pleasures. Decadent, isn't that what the collective calls us?" Darak put the pressure on, wanting to push Jana past her comfort zone just a little.

He slid one hand up to cup her breast through her clothing and squeezed. His gaze held hers as her mouth opened in a little O of surprise mixed with definite pleasure. Darak was too well acquainted with pleasing females—this one, in particular—to mistake that look. He felt a pang of relief. He wasn't pushing too far too fast. She was with him.

So far.

"The collective calls you many things," Jana hedged, holding his gaze, but pointedly not moving out of his embrace.

Darak had to smile. "I'm betting most of them aren't repeatable for a well brought up girl like yourself." He saw her agreement in her eyes. "No matter. I'm sure we've called them a lot worse."

"There's a difference," Jana whispered, moving into his touch as Darak caressed her. "Most of the things they said about Geneth Mar have proven to be a lie. I've seen how you really are. Even if you do fornicate like rabbits on holiday. They were right about that part, at least." She shook her head slightly, sort of disgustedly amused. "But the things you think you know about them..." Remembered horror entered her gaze. "It's worse than you can imagine."

"Shh..." Darak gathered her close, kissing her deeply, wanting to erase the bad memories with good feelings of pleasure. He didn't want her thinking about the past. Only the present. Only the here and now. Only him. And the *Circe*. And her crew.

He lifted her in his arms and sat in his plush captain's chair, with Jana on his lap, still kissing her. When he finally let her up for air, he was glad to see the horror gone from her eyes. Now, those lovely orbs were filled with the fire of passion. The light of desire. He liked seeing that flame in her gaze and wanted to put it there as often as she would let him.

Her attention was caught by Agnor and Seta, still fucking on the nav console. Agnor's robes had fallen away and Darak noted the way Jana's gaze slid over Ag's surprisingly muscular form. Did she linger on his cock sliding in and out of Seta's pussy? Yes, Darak caught her hesitation—her fascination with observing the other couple. It made him think that perhaps Jana was a budding voyeur.

Or maybe she'd just never seen anything like it before in her life. He had little doubt that there was no porn allowed in the collective. And Mithrak, the planet of her birth, had strict morality laws that they actually enforced.

"Do you like his technique?" Darak whispered in her ear, pausing to lick his way around the sexy whorls, making her shiver. "I could spread you out next to her and do you side by side. Would you like that? Maybe we could switch partners mid-fuck. Have a little swinger session?"

"No," she whispered, but he felt the quiver of her body as his hand slipped inside her pants.

"You sure you don't want Agnor's long cock inside you today? The ladies on my crew say he's very good. And Seta certainly seems to enjoy what he's doing."

She shook her head even as she watched the other man work Seta hard. Seta moaned and clawed at Agnor's back, her heels digging into his muscular buttocks.

At that moment, Darak's finger slipped into Jana's wet folds, stroking her clit as she tensed on his lap. Jana looked at him quickly, that lovely shock on her face again, but Darak soothed her, rubbing her clit with a circular motion she seemed to enjoy.

He leaned in and kissed her, then pulled back, sliding his finger deep into her channel, using his thumb to caress her clit. Her eyes widened, and she squeaked a bit. A lovely sound of excitement and discovery. He liked it. And he was absolutely sure she liked what he was doing to her, as well. For one thing, she was creaming all over his hand, making his way slippery and very, very easy. Perfect.

"Look at them, Jana," he whispered, coaxing her to look

away. "See the way he fucks her? See the sparks riding them? You can almost feel the power surge as he slides into her, deeper with every stroke, closer to completion. He's refilling her well of energy, as she is doing for him. The pleasure is fulfilling two very basic needs—that for pleasure and that need all Talents have for energy. The energy of life. Of love. Of the world around us and inside us. The energy we give to each other when we share our bodies and our pleasure." Darak worked her clit as the couple on the console neared their climax. If Darak had his way, Jana would come with them.

Jana squirmed on his lap, but he noticed she didn't look away from the straining couple only a few feet away. They were at the crisis point now, Seta moaning with Agnor's every hard, fast, deep thrust.

"Come with them, Jana," Darak ordered, sliding another finger inside her, pulsing harder, in time with her panting breaths. He felt how close she was. Very close, indeed.

All it would take was just a little more…

Seta cried out, and Jana bit her lips, stifling a moan. She came on Darak's hand, so beautifully. Agnor stiffened, and all three of them found completion. The energy swirled around the bridge, and Darak felt as if he'd accomplished something amazing. Jana had let down another of her many barriers. She had come in public. She had come on command. And she had watched the scene he'd planned out so carefully for her, allowing him to push her limits and proving both to him and herself—he hoped—that she was recovering from the hell the collective had put her through. Little by little, she was healing.

Darak withdrew his hand from her quivering pussy and turned her in his arms, kissing her deeply as she tried to catch her breath. He was so happy for her. So proud of her. So willing to do whatever he could to make her whole.

"You're beautiful, my Jana."

He realized a beat too late that he'd said something wrong. Storm clouds gathered in her eyes as she got off his lap and settled her clothing. She stepped markedly away from him as she spoke in a low tone meant only for him.

"I'm not yours. I'm not anyone's." She turned away and headed for the small console she'd been using while on the bridge. It had become her station, of sorts. But he still heard her next words, and they sent an arrow of pain through his heart for her. "I'm not even my own, anymore."

He was looking for something to say that might mend the wound he'd unintentionally inflicted, but as she took her seat, he heard her final mutter. "But I'll never be theirs again."

Darak wanted to smile, but hid his expression. Jana was fighting back, and he was all for it, even though it meant he'd have to be careful what he said. She was fighting the collective's hold. The physical and psychic bonds had been severed months ago, but Darak knew the damage done to her psyche would take longer to heal. He was happy to see her asserting her own power over her destiny again, even if it was just a muttered promise that she would never allow the collective to get her again.

It was a positive sign as far as he was concerned. Jana's fighting spirit was reemerging. The woman she would have become if not for the collective's intervention was asserting herself, and he couldn't be happier about it. She was making progress. Good progress on all fronts. And he couldn't wait to see what she'd be like once she was well and whole in mind and body once again. He'd bet she'd be hell on wheels, and he was just the man to partner her—if she would have him.

Whoa. Darak stopped his runaway train of thoughts and realized he'd gotten a little carried away. Thankfully, he was distracted by Seta as she righted herself.

"Thanks, Ag, I really needed that," Seta quipped as she kissed Agnor one last time on the lips, helping him back into the robes that had pooled around his ankles.

Jana found herself unable to *not* notice how the other couple carried on after such a blatant display. She found it all so strange. Not only public displays of affection—about which there were strictly enforced laws on her home planet—but public sex seemed to be the norm rather than the exception among the Talents of Geneth Mar.

She'd seen a bit of it while she'd been on the planet, of course. Though judging by the activity of those on this ship, she hadn't seen much at all. Then again, she'd been sequestered much of the time, either in hospital or secreted away on one of her sister's new family's estates.

"It was my pleasure, Seta," Agnor said, drawing Jana's attention once more. "Thank you for the boost in energy, my sweet. It will make sitting this next long watch much easier to bear with such a lovely memory to savor." He kissed her hand gallantly before letting her step away.

Seta smiled at the tall Specitar. "You always were a charmer, Agnor. I love the way you turn a phrase."

Agnor simply bowed his head with a smile as Seta walked off the bridge, grinning and twirling one tendril of her long hair around her finger. Jana noticed the woman wasn't yawning, anymore. In fact, she looked energized, if lazy, in the aftermath of having sex.

She had that smug sort of smile Darak wore occasionally, and Jana had to wonder if Darak had been having sex with the other women—or even the men—on the ship without her knowledge. Then again, Seta had made it a point to state that Darak hadn't had sex with anyone on the ship in a long time. Jana wondered why the other woman had said it. Was it true? If so, what did it mean?

And why did it make Jana's heart feel lighter to think that he hadn't wanted anyone since being with her? It was all so confusing. Frustrating and confounding.

Jana punched up her console with a bit more gusto than normal and was surprised by the flashing message light that greeted her. It wasn't for her alone, though. She looked over at Darak and realized he'd switched on his console, as well, and they both had the same flashing markers.

Her gaze met his. "What is it?" she asked, worried.

"Message from home," he said quietly, shrugging. "Agnor, do you know what this message is addressed to myself and Jana?" Darak asked the comm officer who was just taking his seat.

Jana noticed a little bot had scurried out from storage to clean and sanitize the other console that had just been used as a bed. Very efficient little sex ship, she thought with an inward smirk.

"Yes," Agnor replied, punching up his own display. "The coded transmission came in just a few minutes ago and was routed automatically to your consoles since you were in transit and due here next. They're coded Priority Two."

So, that meant the message was considered urgent, but not to the point of disturbing someone in the bathroom, Jana recalled from her orientation. The various crewmembers had briefed her on their functions under Darak's guidance so she would be more familiar with the ship and its systems. Jana was glad of that preparation now.

Darak shrugged and entered the command that would open the transmission. She watched him read for a moment before doing the same on her console. It was from Jeri. Jana smiled as she saw her sister's face on the small screen.

The small ear device she wore allowed Jana to hear Jeri's words as if she were standing in the room next to her. The infectious joy in her tone was hard to miss and lifted Jana's heart. Jeri was so happy in her new life, and Jana was so happy for her sister. So glad that Jeri had found a way to rise above their terrible beginnings.

"Sorry, guys," Jeri began in her chipper voice. "We're re-routing you. Intel has turned up that only you two can act on. You, Darak, because you command the *Circe* and are fully capable of utilizing all her special abilities. And you, Jana, because of the crystals you still wear. I know you're not going to like this…" Jeri frowned, and Jana worried what could put that look on her sister's face. "You need to go to Liata and talk to a man named Zane."

Liata. The blue agricultural planet she had almost

destroyed.

Jana felt a dread in the pit of her stomach. Although, she knew intellectually that they would probably end up near Liata sooner or later, she hadn't really prepared herself mentally for the idea of coming face to face with her former life as a slave to the collective. As a commander of the armada that had rained death down on an innocent planet from space. As a murderer.

Jana closed the transmission without hearing the rest. She had to think about this first. She had to come to terms with the idea before she could concentrate on whatever her sister wanted her to do there—at the scene of one of her worst crimes.

She felt a warm hand land on her shoulder and looked up to find that Darak had come over to her station, the look on his face full of concern.

"Are you all right?" he asked, his deep voice bringing comfort, even though she knew it shouldn't.

She didn't want to lean on this man any more than she already had. If she was going to get her life back—at least what little was left—she was going to have to stand on her own two feet.

"Fine," she answered quickly. "I'm fine." She thought repeating herself might make it true, but no such luck. Too much had just bombarded her all at once. The sexual display. Darak. Her own forbidden pleasure. Then, this. She stood, shaking off his hand. "I just need a few minutes," she said, feeling panic rise. She needed her shielded sanctuary, and she needed it now.

Darak looked at her with concern, but he let her go. At least, he didn't say anything when she pushed past him and headed out of the hatch and back down the corridor to her room. Thankfully, her hatch wasn't very far from the bridge. Darak had put her next to his own cabin, and the captain was always quartered very close to his command chair.

She palmed open the hatch and stepped into the blessed peace of her room. When she would have shut the hatch behind herself, Darak was there. He'd followed her, after all.

If he was going to argue with her or order her back to the bridge, he could just forget it. She needed minute to breathe. Just breathe.

She felt panic coming on and needed the peace of the reflective field. "I'm switching this on," she warned him.

If he had his own shields up when the field went on, he would feel pain as his own Talent was reflected back at him. It was only right to caution him, but that one warning was all she was willing to give. She hit the command and the protective field went up around her, allowing her to breathe a sigh of relief.

"I'm sorry."

He disarmed her by apologizing. For what, she had no idea, because she hadn't expected an apology from the cocky StarLord.

"Why?" she countered.

"I pushed you too hard, just now. I thought you were all right with it, but…apparently not." He strolled in and sat on her bed, as if he was comfortable in her private space.

She regarded him as her mind spun. She could let him believe her near meltdown was his fault. It would be easier. But it was also cowardly, and Jana Olafsdotter had never been a coward. She wasn't about to start now.

She sighed and took the room's only chair. "It isn't your fault. I just got a little…overwhelmed…by the idea of going back to Liata. I don't remember the planet, you know. I had decided early in my recovery that, at some point in the distant future, I would make an effort to go there on a sort of pilgrimage, so I could see what I had done firsthand. I just didn't expect to do it, right now."

Darak seemed to think on her words before he spoke again, in a low, intimate tone. "Liata was always a possible stop on our journey. Trini, our Loadmaster, is a native of Liata, and we like to stop there when we can so she can see her extended family. We usually pick up some trade for them on the way, though, so likely you wouldn't have had to deal with it until we'd already made a few stops."

"I knew most of that before I ever agreed to this journey," Jana admitted. "I just… This caught me by surprise."

Darak's expression lightened a bit. "Me, too, to be honest. I figured we'd get there when I judged you were ready. Frankly, I'm not sure you're even close at this point, but who am I to question the wisdom of a Sha? Especially one who knows you so well?" Darak shrugged. "You should listen to the rest of the message. Jeri has some advice for you and words of encouragement. She knows what this means to you, and she didn't send her orders lightly. She wouldn't put you through this if it wasn't absolutely necessary. She loves you. She wants only what is best for you."

Jana thought about his words, feeling the truth of them in her soul. "You're right," she agreed at length. "It's just hard for me to be pushed around now that I'm free of the collective. I have these ideas about what I'm doing and where I'm going, and for a few moments, I feel in complete control. Then, something happens, and I realize it's all an illusion. I have no control over anything." Her frustration came out in her voice, she knew.

"If I was a more philosophical man, I'd say something like, we are all merely leaves driven by the wind. All of our best-laid plans are merely illusions, and it's that way for everybody. You're not alone in feeling that you aren't in control of everything. You can't be. Nobody is."

"The Voice is."

"Voice?"

"That's what I call it. The Voice of the collective. The one that whispers." She rubbed her temple, right around one of the smaller glittering bits of crystal. "In here."

Darak moved closer. "You hear them still?"

Jana scrunched her eyes shut. As if that would help. "Sometimes," she admitted in a broken whisper.

It was her deepest fear exposed—that somehow she would be sucked back into the collective. She would rather die than let that happen. The fact that she could still hear them murmuring in the back of her mind, no matter how hard she tried to block them out, petrified her.

"That's why you turn on the reflective field when you're in here," Darak said quietly, figuring out why she hid away whenever she could.

"It's the only thing that shuts them out completely." She decided to just come clean. He had to know that she was the weak link on the *Circe*. If anything happened... "Promise me one thing."

"Anything." Darak's quick response lifted her heart a tiny bit.

"Don't let them take me again. If they try..." She trailed off, unable to put her fears into words.

"It won't come to that." Darak moved closer and took her into his arms. His embrace offered comfort, and she took it gladly.

"But if it does..."

"I won't ever let them take you again," Darak swore it like an oath, and she believed him.

CHAPTER EIGHT

After the change of course, the mood on the ship changed, too. For one thing, the pleasure cruise feel of the voyage took on a much more serious tenor. For another, Jana was put through her paces by Agnor, under Darak's supervision. She was given the first test of her Talent, and Agnor assessed her at Mage level.

It was quite a coup, as she came to understand things. Apparently, nobody passed first test at Mage level unless they were particularly gifted in specialized areas. In such cases, the Talents almost always turned out to be Specitars at their first rank assessment and excelled only in one or two main areas.

But Jana didn't have any of the limitations associated with most Specitars. She did seem to have more proficiency in healing and telekinesis, but she also had moderate telepathy, though it was untrained, and a few other skills. Each day, she spent a few hours with Agnor and Darak—mostly together, though, at times, only one of them would act as her teacher for the day. They trained her relentlessly in the use of her Talent, and little by little, she began to gain skills.

It also became easier for her to use and focus her Talent. There had been pain associated with using it while she was healing, but it seemed she had healed fully now and was able to use her Talent again without fear.

She stayed away from some of the more sexual situations on the ship, opting instead to spend a lot of time alone in her room. The reflective field she invariably put on when she was in there was a blessing. It cut off the murmuring of the collective, which seemed to be getting louder, the farther away they got from Geneth Mar.

Or maybe that was just her imagination. She didn't mention it to Darak or Agnor. They were already watching her a little too closely. She was either in her cabin or in training with one or both of them. In between, she took her turn on bridge watch.

They also spent a bit of time trying to figure out what effect the blue crystals had on her Talent. Agnor had already done some diagnostic tests and come to a few conclusions. The three of them were sharing a meal while they discussed his theories.

"I think it was Jana's strong healing Talent that caused the crystals to fuse to her skin," he said, startling her with the radical idea. Darak nodded, seeming to agree. "Her Talent flowed through the crystal, and the collective's power flowed back toward her from it, as near as I can tell. I think it was the fact that her Talent was so closely linked to the crystal—was being siphoned off by her close proximity to the crystal—that when it hit her body, her natural defenses thought the crystals were part of her. It carried her energy, so her body decided it was part of her body and incorporated it into her skin when her Talent for healing flared out of control in those first few moments after the crystal shattered."

"But I almost died. If my healing Talent kicked in, wouldn't it have healed me completely?" Jana wanted to know.

"Your Talent was untrained, Jana," Darak reminded her. "When Jeri brought you to the *Crice*, most of the shards of crystal had already fused into your skin. I couldn't get them out without causing more damage, but you were bleeding from so many places, they were the least of my concerns.

And then, when there was time to consider removing the shards, they were already so deeply embedded it would have hurt you much more to remove them than to just let them be, for now."

She knew it went without saying that, at some point, if the crystal shards proved to be a problem, they'd have to consider cutting them out of her body. It wouldn't be pretty, and it could kill her, but if the collective could control her through the shards, she would be better off dead, anyway. There were still a lot of unresolved questions around those blue sparklies in her skin.

"It makes sense that, if your healing Talent flared between the time you were impacted by the shards from the control crystal and the time Jeri got to you and brought you back to the *Circe*, it would have resulted in an imperfect healing. It fused the chunks of crystal into your body, as if they had always been a part of it, but because it was an uncontrolled burst, it didn't do much more than that," Agnor explained his theory further.

They had many such conversations in the days that followed as they made their way to the planet she had once decimated. Trini spent more time on the bridge as they approached her home planet. Her excitement to see Liata again was obvious, whereas Jana's dread was something she tried to keep hidden.

When they finally made orbit around Liata, Jana could put off the confrontation no longer. She knew it was cowardly, but she really didn't want to go down to the planet and see the scars of the devastation she had wrought.

But, as Darak had reminded her several times, the message from her sister had been addressed directly to both himself and Jana. She had been more or less ordered by one of the highest-ranking Talents in the universe to revisit Liata. Even though Jeri was her sister, the directive to go down to the planet could not be ignored.

And so it was that Jana stood next to Darak, ready to be translocated down to the surface. It was just the two of them.

Trini had left hours before—when they first made orbit—eager to see her family. Jana, by contrast, had spent the time hiding in her room, dreading the moment Darak would request her presence. Thankfully, they had to wait a few hours, for the planet's rotation to bring daytime in the region where their contact was located.

They had a name and a location, but not much else regarding the mysterious Zane they had been told to meet. Jana assumed Zane was male, but really, this Zane could be anyone.

Darak had greeted her with a smile when she finally dragged herself to the bridge. They would depart from there, leaving Agnor in charge of the *Circe*. Jana faced the viewscreen that showed one of the deep scars her armada had left on the planet below. Her gaze was glued to the visible evidence of destruction, her mind reeling with the undeniable proof of what she had done.

"Hey." Darak's deep voice sounded quietly near her ear. "It'll be all right."

Too late she remembered his empathy. She had no doubt that he was picking up on her emotions at seeing Liata for the first time as a free woman.

"I don't want to go down there," she admitted, feeling shaky.

"I know," he crooned, in a tone one might use to soothe a frightened horse. "But I'll be with you. Trust that Jeri wanted you down there for a reason. She's a Sha now. She sees things that we mere Mages cannot fully understand."

She looked up at him and gave him a lopsided smile. "You're a Master."

It was as if flames reached out and licked her from his gaze. "Glad you realize it."

And, suddenly, she knew they weren't talking about Talent, anymore. They'd roamed into uncomfortable territory, just like that.

"Shall we get this over with?" It seemed easier to get going, rather than deal with Darak's unpredictable mood.

Maybe that had been his intent all along? If so, he was even more devious than she had given him credit for, but in a way, she was glad for his manipulation. Without it, she wasn't sure if she could have found the courage to move forward with their assigned mission.

Darak gave her a formal half-bow and then turned to nod at Agnor. A second later, she was looking at the blue-green surface of Liata.

* * *

Zane was most definitely male. And he was only half Liatan, or so the pale indigo of his skin seemed to indicate. He was definitely part pink and part blue, which made for a stunning purple sheen to his skin that intrigued Jana on some basic level she didn't care to examine too closely.

Darak seemed to get along well with the other man. They had greeted each other with wary suspicion, at first, but over the past few minutes, they had been talking, each seemed to relax by small fractions as basic information was shared and evaluated. They were rapidly building a rapport while Jana watched, intrigued.

She didn't have those kinds of interpersonal skills. In the collective, one simply followed orders. She had never had to think independently about whether or not to trust someone. In the rare moments her own mind was free, she had been too frightened to do much more than just keep it together, without screaming herself hoarse.

As a result, Jana's social skills were next to nil. She had been learning since being freed, but this kind of interaction was well beyond her. She still wasn't sure why Jeri had insisted Jana go down to the planet, but she had to trust that her little sister had a good reason.

Darak and Zane were both built on the large scale Jana associated with warriors. Both were muscular and both moved with smooth, controlled motions. Darak's physique held her rapt attention, but she could appreciate Zane's form, as well. From a purely aesthetic viewpoint, she assured herself.

"You are the Star Killer," Zane surprised her by saying as he finally spoke to her directly.

"The what?" Jana was nonplussed by the title she'd never heard before.

"Jana Star Killer. Your exploits are well known among Wizards. You destroyed Plectar's second sun."

"I did what?" Jana had no true recollection of her years in slavery to the collective, but some of the words Zane spoke brought back fragments of images to her confused mind.

"We heard about Plectar on Geneth Mar," Darak said, standing quietly at her side. "The binary star system was failing, and the second sun would have destroyed all life in its solar system. We'd heard the collective had solved the problem, but we didn't know exactly how. Nobody has destroyed a sun before. It was thought impossible, though there seemed to be no other explanation for what happened there."

"I was there," Zane stated. "My mother is Plectaran. I was visiting her family, trying to figure out how to get them away when the armada arrived. We watched from the surface as best we could, while the Star Killer organized an effort the likes of which I may never see again. She and her twenty ships did a job no one thought possible." Zane looked at her with something like awe. "We still don't know exactly how you did it, but the results were undeniable. Within a week, the planet and all its people had been saved. Plectar went from a desert world to something a lot more comfortable. The changes are still ongoing, even after a decade of work, but the people are prospering as never before. My mother's family, and all those on Plectar, sing praises to the Star Killer."

Zane floored her by bowing his head. Jana didn't know what to do. She looked at Darak for guidance, but he merely shrugged. She looked at him again, more emphatically, and he seemed to finally understand that she had no idea how to deal with something like this.

"Does that mean you'll help us?" Darak stepped in, saving her from having to respond to Zane's outrageous story. "Where do your loyalties lie, Zane?"

She didn't really remember any of it, though vague memories were stirring in the back of her mind. It was as if Zane's words had conjured up images of her past life that even she hadn't known had been in her mind.

Zane straightened from his bow. "I was raised on Liata. I am a Council soldier. My loyalty is to the Council, but my heart lies with the Plectarans, also. I've heard their tales of the Wizards Tithe, and I've seen the way their world is controlled by the collective. If I had been raised there, I would have been part of the Tithe—given to the collective because of my Talent. I am ranked Dominar."

Darak nodded in understanding. "I see."

"No, you don't. Not fully." Zane smiled to soften his words, focusing on Darak. "For all the evil of the collective and the way they subjugate weaker minds, they also do good things from time to time. Saving everyone on Plectar was probably the greatest thing the collective has ever done." Zane's violet gaze shifted back to Jana as if expecting her to say something.

"I don't remember it," she admitted finally. "I'm sorry."

But Zane's reaction was unexpected. He stepped closer to her and took her hands in his.

"I know you were under their control, and for that, I am sorry. But, even within the collective, I have seen instances of free will being expressed. I believe the masters allow it when it is for the good of the collective. Everyone on Plectar remembers you, Jana. You were the voice and the face of the collective during that time. And you were also acting independent of their orders on several memorable occasions, to save lives that they would have sacrificed. We all knew it. And we all knew you would face punishment for what you did to save our people. After the second sun was destroyed, you were recalled, and nobody saw you for months. When you returned to duty, it was clear your memories had been altered. Plectaran agents were watching you from within your army, looking for ways to help you. Plectarans remember."

He squeezed her hands and then stepped back, releasing her. The moment was tense, but she had to be honest.

"I wish I did," she finally said, giving in to the gallows humor that seemed to be her new companion since being freed of the collective.

Zane smiled sadly. "It's all right, milady. We will remember for you, until you reassemble your past—if you are ever able to deal with it all." Zane reached into his pocket and pulled out a data crystal. "This is for you." He handed her the small crystal, much to her surprise. "It is everything the Plectaran underground has on your past history, including detailed reports from within the army that you led."

"But how?" Darak asked, clearly surprised by the turn of events.

Zane grinned at him. "Not every soldier in the collective's massive army is Talented. Most are conscripted from worlds under the collective's rule. Plectar, in particular, is known for its warriors. Many are taken into the collective's army each season. In fact, they are also part of the Tithe. All Talents and as many warriors who want adventure in the stars. They try to watch out for the Plectarian Talents who get sucked into the collective, but it's mostly a lost cause."

"I had no idea," Darak admitted. "But it makes a lot of sense. I'm glad to know that at least one planet that is subject to the collective tries to look out for its people."

"They try," Zane agreed. "But it's not often they can do much for the Talented children who have been taken in the Tithe." Zane shook his head. "The one small comfort they can offer the families is to give them occasional updates on where their children are and what they're doing. The warriors keep up a sophisticated network through which information flows back to Plectar about their missing citizens. And they've been doing it for many years."

"And you're plugged in to this network?" Darak asked.

"Not completely. I was raised here. I'm only half-

Plectaran, though I have made contacts there through my mother's family. In this instance, they reached out to me." Zane pulled another data crystal out of his pocket and handed it to Darak. "This is why you were summoned here. It is a dossier on the man we believe ordered the attack on Liata. His name is Kol, and he is a native of Liata who left to join the collective of his own free will."

Jana cursed. She had been fighting memories of a blue man for most of her recovery, but had comforted herself with the thought that no Liatan—for they were the only blue-skinned race in the stars—would ever be part of the collective on such a high level. It seemed she had been wrong. Her memories started to coalesce around the blue man, and she had a sudden, horrific knowledge of who and what he was.

"He is not merely another member of the collective," she spat. "He is one of the masters. He is part of the Voice."

Zane looked at her with compassion in his violet eyes. "He tested at Mage Master before he left Liata many years ago. It was thought that he would probably rank as high as Vizier some day with his level of raw Talent."

"It makes sense. The collective would probably have the strongest minds on top of the power structure," Darak reasoned.

But Jana was beyond reason. "He is evil," she whispered, remembering Kol's leering blue face above her...as he raped her. Repeatedly. Many times. Over several years.

It all came back to her in a rush, and she staggered. Darak and Zane both reached out to steady her, but she flinched at their touch.

One didn't have to be empathic to realize Jana was hurting. As it was Darak's empathy flared to life as she became more and more distressed. The way she'd rejected his touch hurt him, but her feelings were more important, right now.

Darak looked at Zane accusingly.

"I'm sorry," Zane said. "I'd heard she may have worked

for him, but nobody knew for sure. Kol is very secretive. It's hard to observe him, even for the most highly placed of the Plectaran spies."

"I think I understand," Darak said as comprehension dawned. If Kol was one of the masters who had worked closely with Jana, he was most likely one who had brutalized her, as well. "Is there anything else?" he asked Zane impatiently.

"All the data you need is on the crystal." Zane stepped back.

"Good." Darak moved closer to Jana, signaling the ship. "We're leaving now."

"We will meet again, StarLord. Plectarans remember." Zane stepped back, into the shadows, fading away as the *Circe* responded, bringing them home.

CHAPTER NINE

Jana felt the worry coming from Darak as they translocated back to the ship. Through her own pain, she reached out to him, taking his hand.

"I'm sorry," she whispered when the bridge of the *Circe* reappeared around them.

"None of this is your fault," Darak replied, his gaze holding hers. He took her other hand, much as Zane had done. "You know that, right? You're not to blame for what was done to you without your permission. Or what the collective made you do against your will."

He'd been telling her essentially the same thing for weeks, as had everyone on Geneth Mar who had helped with her recovery, but she still didn't quite believe it. How could she absolve herself of blame when she saw the evidence of what she had ordered done to Liata right there on the viewscreen?

She looked past Darak's shoulder, noting the scars on the surface of Liata that were visible from orbit. She could never forgive herself for that. Nor for the innocent lives lost due to her actions.

"I killed so many here," she whispered brokenly, unable to pull her eyes away from the scarred planet below them.

"And you saved everyone in the Plectar solar system. You heard what Zane said. They think you're a hero, and that you acted on your own initiative to save many the collective would have sacrificed. The woman brave enough to stand up to the collective may not be perfect, but she is brave. Jana, you're still that woman, whether or not you remember every little thing you've done in your past. What matters most is the future. What you do from here on out is the important thing. But you don't have to face the future alone."

Darak moved closer, obscuring her view of the planet below. He stepped right up to her, not quite touching, definitely within the bounds of her personal space. She was forced to meet his gaze.

"I'm with you now, Jana. I won't let anything bad happen to you. Not ever again. Not if I can help it. You don't have to face this alone."

She looked deep into his eyes for a long moment, slowly becoming aware that the rest of the bridge crew was watching them intently. She looked past Darak, to meet the strong gazes of Seta, Agnor, Kirt and Whelan and even Trini, who were all on the bridge for some reason. They nodded at her one by one, silently backing up Darak's words.

The show of unity almost brought her to tears. The *Circe's* crew didn't know her well, but they seemed to trust the judgment of their leader. If Darak was with her, they all were. Just like that. No questions asked.

Jana had the vague recollection of having that kind of loyalty directed at her once. Her memory was in tatters—probably altered with intent by Kol or one of the other masters—but she remembered certain faces. Soldiers. Humans with no discernible Talent. Warriors who had been part of her crew.

They hadn't followed her orders simply out of duty. She had the distinct impression that, after a while, they had followed her for her own sake. The way the *Circe's* crew followed Darak.

Maybe her past wasn't all horror and torture and death. Maybe...just maybe...Darak was right. Maybe the old Jana hadn't been completely bad. Maybe she had done whatever

she could—within the tight confines of the collective's control—to do good things once in a while, along with the bad.

The thought gave her hope.

She consciously straightened her spine.

"I don't know if I can ever be Jana Star Killer again. I don't remember her. But I'll try to be better than I was before. With all of you to help me, I don't see how I can fail at that."

Darak's smile was one of pride mixed with relief. He opened his arms and took her into a hug that warmed her from within. She still felt shaky, but for the first time since waking from her decades-long nightmare, she felt a real sense of hope for the future.

Maybe it wouldn't be as bad as the past. Maybe *she* wouldn't be as bad as she had once been.

* * *

The data crystals from Zane contained a wealth of information. Jana found she could only handle reading small amounts about her past at a time. Most of it, she didn't remember. And a lot of it, she didn't think she wanted to remember.

But she knew she had to face her demons—and her past as part of the collective was the biggest of them—before she could move on. It was slow going, though. The data crystal was filled to capacity, with many detailed reports about Jana Star Killer's actions and activities.

She started with the earliest data and worked her way through it, but she knew it would take time to come to terms with each new discovery. So far, she had read the rather sketchy facts about her initial capture and subsequent forced joining with the collective.

Her early years within the collective were unremarkable, though she started her rise through the ranks after finding success as a platoon leader. It seemed that the un-Talented human troops were routinely assigned a Talented leader who was connected to the collective, so that they could be deployed at the will of the Voice without delay.

It was considered an entry-level position, but after losing most of her platoon during her first real battle, something appeared to have changed within Jana. The Plectaran spies speculated that, even though she was under the collective's control, Jana had found a way to follow their orders in creative ways that led to better outcomes for her platoon, and much less loss of life among her troopers.

That was when the Plectaran soldiers started watching her apparently. There were detailed reports from Plectaran warriors who had served under her command from that point on, as she rose in rank and stature within the army of the collective.

Darak hadn't shared what had been on his crystal, yet, but he'd been closeted in his room with it almost since the moment they'd come back. After he'd calmed her down, they'd shared a meal together, and then, he'd suggested they both get a look at the crystals they'd been given. He'd cautioned her that she should ask for help if she needed it, but also impressed on her that he trusted her to know how much she could handle.

That was a big thing…his trust. His faith in her ability to judge what was best when she didn't even trust herself. If he believed in her, maybe she should believe in herself? It was worth a try. She always had the safety net of being able to call him if she felt the least bit of stress. He was right next door, and she knew he would drop everything and come to her if she needed him.

She hadn't had that kind of faith in someone since her parents. Only her family had ever really been there for her. Until the collective had come calling, of course. They'd killed her parents and torn her away from the only home she had ever known, thrusting her into the middle of a nightmare.

But it was over now. Or it would be as soon as she figured out how to get past the trauma and get on with her life.

Darak was her lifeline. He was there for her. As her parents had been. As Jeri had been. Because…

Because he cared for her?

Jana dismissed the thought. Thinking about such things only confused her. She hadn't had a normal teenage experience. She didn't understand how things happened between male and female. She understood the mechanics, of course, and had learned to enjoy all the things that Darak had shown her, but the emotional part remained elusive. Did he care for her? Did she care for him?

She thought so. Heck, she thought she might even love him. But would he welcome that love? Or did their physical joining mean nothing to him? Merely another experience in a long line of them. She didn't know, and she didn't know if she dared discover the truth.

Which made her a little cranky. And which was also why she limited her exposure to his lovemaking. It was clear he would have welcomed her in his bed all night, every night, but she couldn't bring herself to make a commitment like that without knowing where she stood. And she didn't know how to find that out without looking like a complete and utter fool.

She had read the reports up to the point where she had been given command of her first starship when her stomach growled. Looking at the chronometer, she realized she been at this much too long without a break. She shut down the viewer, leaving the crystal so she could pick up where she'd left off upon her return. Stretching, she walked to her hatch, lowering the reflective field as she left.

It was then she heard the slight increase in volume in the back of her mind. The murmuring of the collective was growing louder. Panic shot through her for a moment before she realized it was still just murmuring. It held no power over her. It didn't even seem to realize she could hear it. It had been the same since she had begun her recovery. It just grew a little louder as they traveled through space, getting closer to areas under collective rule.

So, if the murmuring was getting louder…

Jana rerouted her feet and headed for the bridge rather than the galley. When she stepped onto the bridge, the mood was tense, and Darak was in his command chair, frowning at his personal data screen. He looked up and met her gaze, reserved welcome in his expression, as if he wasn't looking forward to telling her what was on his mind.

She walked right up to him.

"We're going closer to the collective, aren't we?" Her tone was challenging, but she didn't wish to recall her words.

It was time she began to stand up for herself. The warrior Jana she had been reading about didn't take shit from anyone—including her so-called masters in the collective. At least, she did what she could to circumvent their crappy orders and find ways to keep her men alive while still achieving the objectives set out by the Voice.

That's what the reports she'd read so far had told her. The new Jana found solace in that small rebellion of her younger self. It made her feel better to know that even while under their control, she'd found ways to thwart them. Small ways, to be sure, but at least she'd put up a fight and saved lives in the process. That had to count for something, right?

"Yes." He answered her challenge simply, with no subterfuge.

"Why?"

"Several reasons, actually." Darak sat back and rubbed his hand over his stubbly chin. He hadn't taken time to groom himself, which told her a lot. Whatever had been on the crystal he'd gotten had to be very important.

"Will you tell me?" She held her breath, waiting for his answer.

"There are few secrets on the *Circe*," he replied almost automatically. "We're all here because we're working toward the same goal. So, yes, I will tell you. In fact, I'd planned to hold a crew briefing so everyone knows what we're getting into. Agnor…" he turned his attention to the tall man at the comm station, "…ask everyone to come up here for a few minutes."

Agnor nodded and turned back to his panel to issue the communication to the rest of the crew. Within a minute, they began to arrive. Seta was first, yawning and wearing a see-through nightie. The two yeomen entered next, both in loose pants with stretchy shirts that showed off their muscular physiques. Trini was last, but she was at least fully dressed, having been on duty in the hold, doing inventory from the looks of the datapad in her hands, the scanner on her belt, and the stylus stuck behind her ear.

"Due to the intel we picked up on Liata, I've plotted a course for Mithrak."

Jana gasped, and a few eyes turned to her in sympathy. She had been born on Mithrak. She had been stolen from Mithrak. And she'd never been back to the place of her greatest joy and her greatest sorrow.

"The Liatan governing council believes that the reason they were attacked is due solely to one of their own who took off and joined the collective of his own free will," Darak went on.

It was Trini's turn to gasp. She was a native of Liata and probably found it hard to believe one of their own would send an armada to destroy their home planet.

"Our target's name is Kol. He's Liatan, so therefore has blue skin. There are no current surveillance images of him. He's very careful about being seen. But we've learned that he's leading the Wizard cull on Mithrak over the next three weeks. If we can pin him down, we have orders to attempt capture and return to Liata so he can stand trial. If we can't manage a capture, we are authorized to kill. His crimes against his home planet have earned him a death sentence."

"They have proof?" Trini asked, her hand trembling.

"Irrefutable proof," Darak answered. "I'm sorry, Trin. I know Liatans are generally pacifists. This man is a threat that your government wants gone."

"If we don't know what he looks like, how do we identify him? We can't just go shooting every blue person on the planet. Liatans like to travel. There's bound to be a few there besides the one we're looking for," Seta pointed out.

Darak turned to look at Jana. "I was hoping…"

"I can identify him," Jana said in as strong a voice as she could manage. "In fact, I can do a computer sketch of his face as I remember it. It may not be exact, but it'll be good enough to start the search."

Darak smiled at her for the first time since she'd stepped onto the bridge. It was a small smile, but a smile nonetheless, and it warmed her.

"All right," Darak recaptured everyone's attention. "Seta, I want you to check my nav calculations once you wake up a bit, then you can go back offshift. Trini, we'll need to change the ship ID and find something in the hold that might possibly pass for trade on Mithrak. Ag, you're on our alternate personal IDs. Do at least one for everyone, just in case. Jana's working on the sketch, and I want you two…" he pointed to the two yeomen, "…to calibrate the guns and check the weapons systems."

Jana was hearing things she hadn't truly comprehended about the little cargo vessel. For one thing, it was armed. Now, the presence of the young men made more sense. She'd wondered what their duties entailed, but if there were guns, they'd need someone to fire them during battle. Not everything could be left to a computer—even a really good one was no match for the computing power of the human mind. And if those minds were Talented, as she knew both yeoman's were, then the possibilities of successful targeting increased exponentially.

The fact that everyone seemed nonplussed at the idea of changing the ship's ID along with their own personal IDs also told her something. She'd assumed Darak and this ship operated as some kind of intelligence gathering group for the Council. She hadn't realized just how actively they participated in the spy game. The *Circe*, in truth, was a full-fledged spy vessel.

Jana grinned as she sat at her console, pulling up the items she would need to create an image of the blue man she remembered from her nightmares. It wasn't a pleasant task, but if she could put a stop to Kol, the bastard, she would put every effort into the task. He needed to be stopped. And he needed to pay for what he'd done. Preferably by her own hand.

Only then, she feared, would she be able to bury the past. With him.

Within a few hours, Jana was finished with the sketch. It was as good as she could make it working from hazy memory and using the computer for assistance. She sent the image to all personnel after showing it to Darak first.

Darak had stared at the image of Kol's face for a long time, his expression hard. She knew he was memorizing it, possibly looking for some sign of how such an outwardly plain-looking fellow could be so cruel and power-mad. Jana had wondered the same thing whenever her mind was free of the collective. Which, mercifully, hadn't been all that often.

For when Kol cut her off from the collective, it was to play his sick games. He would use the time off the grid to rape her. Sometimes, he held a knife to her throat. Sometimes, he cut her. Once, he'd beaten her.

That time, she recalled now, at least one of the soldiers who stood guard inside the "playroom", as Kol called it, had to be restrained by one of his compatriots. Kol hadn't seen it, but Jana remembered the guards behind Kol moving—one trying to come to her aid while the other held him back, shaking his head furiously.

Even then, she had understood why the guard's impulse had been thwarted. She'd wanted that guard to help her, but she knew if he stepped out of line, Kol would have him killed. His kindness would be repaid with death—his and possibly his entire platoon's. Kol had that kind of power over them all. It would do no good to go against his wishes.

But Jana also remembered that after Kol had finished with her, that guard had picked her up and taken her to a healer. His face was the last she'd seen before sliding into unconsciousness, and when she'd awoken, she was back in the collective.

She still remembered that guard's face. She had known his name, too, but it escaped her, at the moment. Her memories were coming back in bursts, but they weren't always complete. Perhaps, in time, she would get the rest of the memories back. Perhaps not. At this point, she wasn't sure if she really wanted to remember everything.

Then again, that guard had been kind to her. He'd had nothing to gain by treating her with gentle hands. He could just as easily have tossed her to the healers and turned away. But he'd stayed while they worked and watched over her until she lost consciousness. He might even have stayed after that. She didn't know. But he'd cared when Kol had hit her. She'd seen his involuntary move and the deliberate way he'd been stopped by his fellow. At least that one soldier had had some compassion for her. So, maybe it wasn't all bad.

After she finished with the sketch, there seemed little for Jana to do. Everyone was busy with the tasks Darak had set for them. She considered going back to her cabin to read more about her past life, but she wasn't really sure she wanted to know more, right now. Her mind was overflowing with everything she'd already learned. She needed a little bit of time to integrate all the new data flowing into her brain.

"Jana." Darak's voice came to her as she was considering her options for what to do next. She turned from her console on the bridge to look at him.

He was much closer than she'd thought. She looked up to meet his gaze as he stood only a few feet away from her.

"There's something we need to discuss. Have you eaten recently?" His expression seemed open enough, though she worried about what he might want to talk to her about in private.

"I could eat," she said, standing and securing her station. They walked together, off the bridge and down to the galley.

He served them both before he started on the topic he wanted to discuss. Jana realized she was quite hungry, after all, and nibbled on the meal he'd set before her while he got down to business.

"Jana, I think you realize your appearance is going to make it almost impossible to disguise you adequately for this mission. The crystals in your skin can't be hidden, and we can't take the chance that members of the collective will recognize you. You were one of their top ship captains. A lot of people will have seen your face." Darak laid out the facts while they ate.

"I can't argue with your logic," she admitted. "If nothing else, the crystal shards are a liability. I can hide the ones on my body under clothing, but the ones on my face..." She trailed off, letting her fingers glance over the permanent jewelry embedded in the skin of her face.

"Right," Darak agreed. "Which is why I want you to stay on board when I go down to the surface of Mithrak." He looked up from his meal and sought her gaze.

"I may not remember much about my previous life, but I do remember that I'm not used to inactivity. If there's a mission happening, I like to be in the middle of it," she stated truthfully. "But I do realize why you're asking this. Truly, I do. You want to keep me safe and your concern is something I value highly. It's been a long time since anybody's cared about my welfare, Darak, and I treasure that. But I can't help but think that you might need me along with you on this mission. For one thing, I know how the collective works. I can tell you what they're going to do even before they do it— both from experience and because..." She took a deep breath before revealing the discovery she'd been fighting against. "Because the closer we get to them, the louder the Voice is at the back of my mind. I can hear them, Darak. They're getting clearer all the time."

Darak frowned and reached across the table to take one of her hands in his. "Is it dangerous? Will you fall into the collective again?"

"I don't believe so," she answered. "I can hear them, but it's as if they are totally unaware of me. Maybe the crystals block them from recognizing my mind as a separate entity. I don't know. But whatever it is, this doesn't feel the same way the Voice used to feel in my head."

"Describe it for me," Darak prompted, not unkindly.

"Before, the Voice was a compulsion. Something I had to obey no matter what. I had no free will of my own, and it was aware of me in every way. It could rip apart my mind and rifle through my thoughts whenever it wanted, or it could take me over completely—which it did for long periods of time." She shuddered remembering the oily feeling in her mind after those instances. "Now, it's separate. Like something I'm overhearing that has no idea I'm there at all. I feel no connection to it. No need to obey it. I can just hear it and observe from afar. It seems to have no interest in me."

"But that could change, couldn't it? If Kol or someone like him saw you. Couldn't they use that connection to try to enslave your mind again?" Darak insisted.

"I know they would try, but I think the crystals would stop them. I think they protect me in some way. Isolate me from the collective while still allowing me to hear the Voice."

"What is it saying?" Darak's gaze was intense.

"Mostly indistinct murmuring right now, but occasionally I hear words. I believe as we get closer, it will become clearer. I can tell you that earlier, when I was working on Kol's likeness, I heard a directive to burn something. A farmhouse, I think. The Voice sounded angry. Like it had been thwarted in some way."

Darak sat back in his chair, regarding her steadily. "We'll be in range in the next few hours, for long scan. I'll ask Agnor to check for any fires—or heat signatures—on the ground. Maybe you can help us pinpoint a location to start our search for Kol." Jana nodded, wanting to help in any way she could. "And I want Agnor to run a few more tests. If your abilities are changing, it would be best to analyze the nature of the change. For one thing, we need to determine if this new skill is coming from within yourself, or being imposed from the outside."

"You mean the collective, right?" She shook her head. "I don't think so, but you're wise to check. I have no objection to more tests. I'd like to be as certain as I can, too. I'd rather die than go back to the collective." She swallowed hard and steeled herself to ask something of him that she had been dreading. "If it comes to that, Darak, I want your promise. Shoot me yourself before you let me go back to them."

Darak scowled. "I've told you already—it won't come to that. Which is why I want you here, safely aboard the *Circe*. She has cloaking technology unlike any other ship in space, right now. Everything on her is cutting edge technology. She will keep you safe, even when I can't."

"But what if—"

He cut her off. "No, Jana. If I have to make it an order, I will. Hells, if I have to tie you up myself, I'll do it. I don't want you coming down to the planet. Let us handle this. Just do what you can from up here to keep us informed of anything you might hear."

Jana didn't like it, but finally she nodded her agreement. "I can do that."

"Good. Now, when was the last time you slept?" Darak rose from the table, disposing of their trash as he escorted her toward the hatch.

"I don't really remember. A lot has been happening. I don't even know what shift it is." She laughed at her own absent-mindedness, and Darak joined in with a chuckle.

"You know, I don't either." He ran one hand through his hair. "I think we both need some downtime."

She paused in front of her cabin's door, suddenly realizing that things were changing rapidly. He was going down to the surface of Mithrak, and there was a chance he might never come back. Something inside her refused to believe it, but another part worried. And yet another part wanted to grab what little happiness she could before everything went to hell.

Jana stepped closer to him as he stood with her in front of her hatch. "If I ask nicely, will you come inside?" She didn't quite know where the words were coming from, but from the widening of his eyes, they seemed to have the desired effect.

"Are you sure?" His voice had dropped to a low, seductive rumble.

"No, but I know I want you with me tonight. Or today. Or whatever time it is." She smiled and stepped into his embrace, reaching up to kiss him gently. "I didn't like remembering Kol. Come help me erase him from my mind again. Replace the bad memories with good ones."

"I can do that," he promised with a sexy growl in his voice. He kissed her right there in the hallway, pushing her back up against the bulkhead.

The first touch of his lips erased any lingering bad memories, just as she'd hoped. Even more, Darak's kisses had a way of making her forget everything but the sensations he aroused in her awakening body.

It wasn't until one of the young yeomen passed by, making enough noise to shake Jana out of her reverie, that she realized they were still in the public corridor. She pulled away, shocked to find Darak had her breast in his hand, thankfully under her shirt. The yeoman hadn't seen her flesh, though he had to know what they'd been doing.

Even after all her exposure to the casual sharing of pleasure aboard the *Circe*, Jana still felt uncomfortable. And, if she was honest, a little naughty...in a good way. But she couldn't just drop the strict ideas she'd been raised with in a few short days.

Jana palmed the locking mechanism, and the hatch slid open next to them. Daring greatly, she dragged a very willing Darak by the collar into her room and made sure the hatch closed and locked behind them. Darak was chuckling when she turned to look up at him.

But he stopped laughing when she dropped her clothing, bit by bit, leaving a trail of garments from the hatch to the bed. His penetrating gaze followed her every move, and when she was fully naked, she struck a pose for him, crooking one finger in invitation.

Darak stripped off in record time, following the short path

she had forged, his clothing falling on top of hers. When he reached her side, he was as naked as she, and he wasted no time pressing his body against hers.

His hard muscles and slightly rougher skin made her feel soft and womanly. The almost reverent way he touched her made her feel like a precious jewel he wanted to admire and pamper. When he lifted her in his arms and placed her down on the bed, she felt as if she was flying for a moment out of time, safe in his strong arms.

His lovemaking was soft and gentle, this time. There was no rush once he'd brought their bodies together. He took his time arousing her in every way. He spent long minutes worshiping her breasts, working his way slowly down her abdomen, pausing to swirl his tongue lightly around her navel.

And then, he went lower. He caressed her legs apart, kissing his way between her thighs until she moaned in pleasure. His tongue played over and within her folds, setting up an expert rhythm that brought her to a small completion within moments. But he didn't let her go. He started over, bringing her higher than ever before, reigniting the fires even hotter, until finally, she was ready to burst into a fireball of need.

Only then did he join their bodies together, taking her with that same gentle strength that made him so different from any other being she had ever known. Only Darak had showed her that sex could be tender as well as passionate. Only Darak had ever wanted her to enjoy the act as much—if not more—than he did. Only Darak made her feel...loved.

Whether it was real or not, she felt the caring of his heart for her with her empathic senses. In this moment, for this small space of time, she was important to him.

That meant something.

Even if it turned out to be false in the morning, right now was what mattered to her. It mattered that the man who took her body also cared for her enjoyment, for her sanity, for her comfort. Darak felt those things. She knew he put her pleasure above his own.

And for that, she would always cherish this special time with him.

CHAPTER TEN

It was hard to leave her. Jana had come to mean so much to him in so short a time. She was fast becoming the center of his universe. But she still carried a heavy burden on her shoulders and in her mind. Darak would do anything to alleviate her pain. Including hunting down the man who had hurt her so badly. Darak hoped Kol would resist arrest. He was itching for a reason to kill the other man.

But first, he had to find him. Agnor had found evidence of several fires on the surface of the planet in recent days. Apparently, the Wizards liked to burn out the homes of those who disagreed with him, or tried to keep their Talented children hidden. From all accounts, that's what had happened to Jana and Jeri's home.

Their parents had been killed and the farm burnt to the ground. Jeri had escaped by hiding with the herds of horses their family had raised. Jana hadn't been so lucky. She'd been swept up in the Wizard's cull—which is what they called the annual visit by a group of red-robed Wizards on Mithrak.

On Plectar, Darak now knew since meeting Zane, they called it the Tithe, and different traditions had grown up around the collection of Talents by the collective. On Plectar, they took both warriors and Talents. On Mithrak, only Talents, since the native population was mostly herders and farmers.

The fires were a good clue about where to start looking for Kol. Where there was a Talent being collected, Kol would probably be close at hand, ready to subdue the young mind and subvert it to the collective. Such a task would require a powerful mind and couldn't be left to thralls or soldiers. It would have to be done by one of the puppet masters.

Darak had chosen to take Seta and Agnor with him down to the planet. If nothing else, Seta was perfect for distracting men—and many women, too. A former Virulan sex slave, Seta has certain skills and a willingness to show her body that would easily scandalize the straight-laced natives of Mithrak.

And Agnor, though taller than most people, blended in very well when he chose to be stealthy. He had a way of moving silently and not attracting attention that was the exact opposite of Seta's skills. She was all about standing out. Agnor was good at concealment. Darak wasn't sure what would be called for, so he took them both with him.

Parting from Jana was painful but necessary. She meant too much to him for him to risk her safety on this mission. But he hated leaving her behind.

She was just starting to come into her own. Her true personality was beginning to emerge, and he liked Jana on every level. She stimulated him in every way possible, including intellectually, which wasn't something he found very often. Her strength of character was impressive. She had let him peruse the data crystal Zane had given her while she was in the shower, and he'd zeroed in on the final missions she had run for the collective.

She'd been rejecting the collective's power over her as much as she could. He could see that in the reports from the Plectaran soldiers. And it was clear those same soldiers admired her leadership. They were loyal to her—not necessarily the collective.

Darak had to stop thinking about her, though. He was on a mission, in the middle of enemy territory for all intents and purposes. Mithrak may not like the way the Wizard's collective harvested their children, but Mithrakians had no choice. Their planet was firmly under the control of the collective and had been for many years. Darak would find few friends here if they knew he had come from a Council world.

Mithrak was a place of moral strictures and social laws that made no sense to someone raised in the permissive society of Geneth Mar. Mithrakians would never accept the morals—or lack of them, as they saw it—of Council Talents. They preferred the rigid rule of the collective, which did not encourage or showcase what went on behind closed doors.

What had been done to Jana would never be common knowledge, though it probably had happened to many others unfortunate enough to gain the notice of one of the more perverted puppet masters. Mithrak simply didn't know that their children could be abused in such a way. In fact, once the children were taken, they were never seen again on Mithrak.

Darak wasn't concentrating when he ran afoul of a red-robed Wizard on the street of a small town. It wasn't the blue skinned bastard he was after, but one of the others. Darak went quietly when the Wizard demanded his ID credentials and detained him until his status could be clarified. A platoon of soldiers backed up the lone Wizard, and Darak realized he was well and truly caught. For now.

Not even two hours on the surface of Mithrak, and he'd already been arrested. *Good going, StarLord.*

* * *

"What do you mean he's been arrested?" Jana jumped out of her chair, shouting at Agnor through the comm.

Trini and the two yeomen were on the bridge with her since the other three were on the surface. She hadn't been expecting Agnor to comm, but had been standing by, just in case.

"I'm not totally sure what happened. We dare not use our Talents while under such close observation, so I can't 'path him to ask. I only know that Seta saw him being arrested by a platoon of warriors under the direction of a brown-skinned man in a red robe."

"So, at least he didn't run straight into Kol," Jana muttered. "But red robes are bad. They indicate higher-ranking Wizards. They usually carry control scepters, like I did."

"You were one of these red robes?" Agnor asked, seeming unable to stop his innate curiosity.

"No. Wrong branch. I was strictly military. It takes a different set of skills and inclinations to be in collections. But the control crystals were only given to those of high enough power and rank to use them. In collections…well…those Talents want to be there. They want to be part of the collective and are actively seeking promotion to higher ranks. Most of them aspire to be part of the Voice, and probably are given some of that authority when they're on collection runs, but I have no idea how that sort of thing is decided long term. I had the crystal only so I could complete my missions. They didn't trust me with any more than that. I was merely a handy tool to be used and discarded. The red robes are active players in the political game." She frowned. "Darak being taken by one is a really bad thing. At some point, they'll try to probe his mind."

"And find his shielding," Agnor finished the thought that spelled doom for Darak and his mission.

"I'm coming down," Jana said decisively.

"I don't think—" Agnor began, as did the others who were listening in on the bridge, but she cut them all off.

"That's Darak down there. His life is in the balance, and I can help. I have to try."

Nobody argued any further. Jana had already dressed ready for action. She'd taken a few things from the armory and ordered appropriate clothing from the fabricator hours ago, including a scarf she could wrap around her head, to hide part of her face and the small crystals embedded there. She had wanted to be prepared, just in case. It looked like her preparations had not been in vain.

She was ready to go immediately and didn't see the sense in waiting. She stepped onto the pad and gave the nod. Within seconds, she had translocated down to the planet, inside the humble hotel room that Agnor had rented.

"Where's Seta?" she asked, noting they were alone in the single room.

"She went out to try to help Darak, but she's been gone too long," Agnor admitted. "And I don't think this location will remain safe much longer. We should go."

"No." Jana touched Agnor's arm, stilling his motion. "You should go. Back to the ship."

"I can't leave Darak—" he objected, but she cut him off.

"Agnor, look." She let go of his sleeve and ran a hand over her nearly braided hair, making sure it was still perfectly in place. Just the way Mithrakian natives liked it. "You don't fit in down here. I do. This is my homeworld. I know how things work here. Or at least I did. And I look like the natives. You don't. Frankly, you stick out like a sore thumb here. Even you can't hide the fact that you're a foot taller than everyone else. If you stay here, you'll be the next one singled out and probably arrested. Tensions flare during the cull. Strangers are always mistrusted, but even more so during the cull."

"But I have to help free him."

"You do. And you can do that best from the *Circe*. I'll need intel, and frankly, Trini and the boys can't handle comm and scan the way you can. They need a leader up there, and I need you up there. Go. Be my eyes in the sky. I'll get Darak out and find out where Seta's gone. Better yet…" She pulled two transponder dots out of her pocket. "I'll retag them so you can translocate them out of trouble."

They both knew the first thing that would be done upon arrest was a nullification pulse that would render any retrieval tech on their bodies inoperative. They'd have to be re-tagged in order for the translocation device to locate them without use of a pad.

"You planned ahead." Agnor looked at her with new

respect.

"It's my nature. I was ready for action ten minutes after you left the bridge. Just in case." She cracked a small smile. "I'm a warrior, Agnor. I'm better suited to this particular mission than you are. Let me do my thing. You know it's the logical choice."

Agnor looked at her for a long time as if weighing his thoughts. Finally, he nodded. "I will go back up, for now. I will follow your transponder signal and watch your progress. Comm when you can and let us know what's going on. I can come right back down if you need me."

"Thank you for your trust," she said formally. "I'll find them and get them back to you." She didn't know if she'd live through this mission, but she was determined to rescue Darak and Seta, or die trying.

Agnor translocated out, and Jana left the hotel as quickly as possible.

And not a moment too soon. As she walked out, a platoon of soldiers marched in and demanded entry to the room she had just vacated.

Jana kept to the shadows as much as possible as she walked down the street. This wasn't the town near her old home, but it looked similar, and the smells of this planet were exactly as she remembered them. Horses, dust and green, growing things.

She tried to quell the memories as best she could, concentrating on her mission. The detention center wasn't hard to find. It was the same as the one she remembered seeing on the occasional trips she had made into town with her father and mother. It was a squat, black building with no windows and the shield of the enforcers over the door.

Jana took up a position across the street, in a small café. She ordered a light meal and sat at one of the outdoor tables where she could observe without being too visible. Luckily, this café was moderately busy and she did her best to blend into the crowd.

Her seat was on the edge of the rectangular grouping of

tables spread across the front of the café. She had her back to the front wall of the building and was protected on one side by the slightly protruding wall of the building next door. There were thick shallu vines growing up the side of the building beside her that looked strong enough to climb, should the need arise, and she was careful to sit with her bejeweled right side, still hidden by the scarf and her clothing, angled away from the street, just in case.

She sipped her drink as she nibbled on the meal that held the spices and flavors of her youth. It wasn't as good as her mother's cooking, but nostalgia threatened with each bite. Until she saw the soldiers.

Two platoons of soldiers surrounded a man in a red robe as he neared the detention center. It wasn't Kol. From her vantage point, she could see the man had brown skin, not the blue of Kol's. This one, then, might be the one who had gotten Darak arrested in the first place. He'd probably come back to question his prisoner, which was something Jana could not allow.

She tried to tune in the murmuring of the Voice that had gotten clearer and more distinct in the back of her mind. Before, it had been a nuisance. Something to tune out. But now, it might tell her things she needed to know.

There weren't too many Talented minds actually here on Mithrak right now that were actively part of the collective. Maybe a few dozen. And not all that powerful. There were a few lower-level soldiers and platoon leaders—as she had once been—relaying orders to the non-Talented warriors. Then, there were a few of the red-robed climbers who were trying to curry favor with the leader of this expedition.

It was the leader—Kol—who she wanted to kill.

But first, she had to free Darak if at all possible. Listening intently to the murmur of voices in the back of her mind, she didn't hear Kol's voice in the mix. Perhaps he was operating outside the collective, right now. Or perhaps he was some distance away, on the full night side of the planet, and sleeping. The rotation of the planet would bring daylight and her opportunity to kill him when he woke, if that was the case.

For now, she had to tune into the red robe that had just walked into the detention center.

Once she focused her thoughts, it was easier than she ever would have expected.

The crystals in her body tingled slightly as she used them to focus her energy. She'd thought about doing so many times, but had never dared while aboard the ship. For one thing, she wasn't sure what would happen and didn't want to intrude on the privacy of the crew.

She'd been right to hesitate. With just the smallest amount of effort, she was connected with every Talented mind on Mithrak. Just a little. Both those in the collective, and those young, terrified minds that had been culled this year.

And, much to her surprise, a much larger group of older minds that had somehow escaped the cull to live in secret. They were just as afraid, but a little more secure because they were older and had lived through the cull before.

She dismissed all of those minds, looking for two in particular. First and foremost, she wanted to focus on the red-robed Wizard who was probably going to question Darak any moment now. She also searched for the puppet master. Kol. He had to be there somewhere, but she didn't sense him.

No matter. She would find him, eventually. And when she did, she would kill him.

For now, with only a tiny bit more effort, she was able to listen in on the thoughts of a red robe named Geranth. He was a native of Sheshur Four and had been part of the collective since he was a young man. He'd joined voluntarily, eager to gain position by giving over control of his high-level Talent.

He had risen far on Kol's coat tails, but he knew he needed to do something bigger to attract the kind of attention he needed to advance. Geranth thought perhaps the outworlder he'd had detained earlier might be his ticket. There was something *off* about the man. Something he couldn't name, but would discover given enough time.

He would split the man's mind if he had to. With the power of the collective behind him and the blue crystal scepter in his hand, he had enough power to rip open all but the most powerful minds. Geranth looked forward to hurting the man—whether he was Talented or not. Geranth enjoyed inflicting pain. Which is why he liked serving Kol so well.

Jana had heard enough. She finished her meal and stood, thanking the server with the proper amount of Mithrakian politeness. Setting off down the street, she circled around the detention center again, looking for the back entrance. There had to be one. All detention centers had a back way in for deliveries, workers to come and go unobserved, and the occasional high profile detainee that they didn't want to parade up and down the main street.

Finding what she was looking for, Jana was pleased to see a delivery in progress. She was able to slip in, almost completely unnoticed. The few that did note her passing were easily convinced, with the slightest touch of her mind, that all was well and she belonged here.

Although she had touched on Darak's mind before, she had not risked contacting him. For one thing, she knew he was going to be difficult about her presence on planet. For another, she didn't know if Geranth or one of the other stronger minds on Mithrak could pick up on her use of power. If they were working in collections, they probably had just those sorts of skills, in order to detect hidden Talents. She had to tread lightly. So far, the tiny use of her crystals didn't seem to be arousing any sort of notice.

But the same couldn't be said of her presence in the cellblock. The warriors had formed a cordon around the cells, and there was no way in without going past them. She had to find some credible ruse.

A tray of food caught her attention, and she picked it up, heading straight for the entrance to the cellblock, as if on an errand. When she made to move past the large man who was blocking the entry, he grabbed her arm, and her scarf became dislodged enough that he could see her face.

She looked up to meet his eyes and saw…recognition.

"Star Killer," he whispered.

The fact that he hadn't immediately called for support from his fellow warriors, or his platoon leader—who was undoubtedly a lower-level Talent connected to the collective—gave her hope. She met his gaze steadily.

"I was, but no longer. I am a free woman now, and I have come for what is due me." She tried to explain her presence in words the warrior would understand.

Jana was beginning to remember her time spent among the warrior class and the armies of the collective. She remembered their code of honor. It hadn't been something the collective had fostered. No, the code of honor was something the soldiers brought with them from their home planets and adapted to life in the stars. They understood vengeance. They also understood the need for retribution.

She was banking on the fact that the non-Talented soldiers of the collective had among them certain factions of which the collective was not even aware. The Plectaran spies, for example. Their reports had called her Star Killer. The soldier holding her arm used the same name. If he wasn't part of the spy ring, he at least had heard of her exploits from them.

It was also possible that this man had been part of her armada. He might even have been under her direct command, for all she knew. She didn't remember every face. Hells, she didn't even remember most of them. Her memories were still hazy, but she recognized the look in this man's eyes. It was one of respect, mixed with a bit of fear.

He seemed to consider for a moment. Then, he spoke in a hushed tone.

"Do you come to kill Geranth?"

She knew Geranth's death would have repercussions for these men. They could well be executed for not protecting such a senior member of the collective. She didn't want that. She didn't want to hurt even more people. Kol was the only one she wanted dead.

"I have no quarrel with Geranth save that he holds a friend of mine prisoner. I have come for the prisoner. If possible, I will leave Geranth alive, so that you do not pay the consequences for my actions."

The soldier seemed to consider her words a moment longer, then he released her arm. She was surprised, but managed to hide her reaction.

"They said you were always careful of those under your command," the soldier shocked her by saying. "I am glad to see the reports are true. You may pass, and if you can spare Geranth, I will count it a favor. I have no desire to see myself and my men punished. But do what you must, Star Killer. We owe you for not spending our lives like spare change."

Jana didn't know how to answer. She was touched deeply by the warrior's words. She couldn't thank him, but she could give him something...

"If ever you break free and need a place, look up Jeri Olafsdotter on Geneth Mar. Tell her you knew her sister. She will take you in and give you a place where you will not be mistreated."

The warrior nodded to her, acknowledging her words. "Go now, before others become suspicious."

He didn't mean his platoon. She knew their bonds were those of brothers. He was talking about the platoon leader— the low-level Talent that issued the orders direct from the collective. He or she wasn't here at the moment, but Jana knew that could change.

"Thank you," she whispered as she went past the soldier and into the cellblock.

She ditched the plates on the tray as soon as she realized the cells were empty, save for the one that currently held Darak. It looked like Geranth was just getting started with his questions from outside the door of the cell when Jana hit him from behind with the empty tray.

He crumpled and fell. She reinforced his concussion with a mental command sent through the stones in her skin that ordered him to sleep. His mind—strong as it was—was no match for hers, amplified by the blue crystals. He was going to have a fuzzy head and one hell of a headache when he finally woke up. They would be long gone by that time, of course.

Darak looked at her from behind the barred door of his cell. "What are you doing here?"

"What does it look like? I'm rescuing you," she quipped, stripping off Geranth's robe.

"What about the lock?" Darak quirked one eyebrow at her.

Truthfully, she hadn't thought that far ahead, but in the old days, she used to be able to...

"Stand back," she warned before focusing her power on the electronic lock.

A sizzling noise preceded the tiny puff of smoke, and then, the door clicked open. Jana had always had a way with electronics. She was glad to see that skill hadn't gone away.

"Put this on," she said, thrusting the red robe at him.

Geranth had worn the pointy hat, as well, which obscured his face from the sides and back. Only someone looking at him straight on would realize Darak wasn't the same man who had entered the cells minutes before.

"What about the soldiers?" Darak asked as he hastily climbed into the garments.

"They let me through. Apparently, at least one of them remembers the Star Killer fondly." She helped him fasten the hat, arranging the flaps over his back and shoulders. "Order them to stay and guard the prisoner. A small show of telekinesis is probably in order, as well. Geranth there was the only red robe in this quadrant. I don't think any of the others will notice a small burst of power this far away. Especially since Geranth is supposed to be testing candidates from the cull."

Darak helped her drag Geranth's unconscious form into the cell and arrange him on the small bed. The blanket they put over him completed the disguise. He was the prisoner now. Sound asleep on his cot.

"You go first, Jana," Darak said as they neared the entrance. "I'll be right behind you if there's trouble."

She didn't like it, but knew it would look strange for Geranth to be walking with a servant. She leaned up and kissed his cheek before heading back the way she had come. She remembered to take the tray with her, along with the stuff that had been on it, as she made her way back through the line of guards.

Jana looked around, glad to see the platoon leader had not arrived. The only people there were the ones she had seen before—the soldiers who had let her pass. They must have been talking amongst themselves because, just as she was about to clear the area, one older warrior at the end of the phalanx nodded at her.

She saw the movement and looked up quickly to assess what it meant. The older man's blue eyes met her gaze, and he had tears in them that he did not try to hide.

"Bless you, Star Killer, for saving our families on Plectar."

Jana jumped a bit, surprised by his open speech. The soldiers were human. No Talents among them. And they all seemed cut from the same block. They were all natives of Plectar, like so many in the collective's army.

"We do what we must for the good of all," she replied, not wanting to pretend his thanks didn't matter.

Of all people, Plectarans would understand what she meant. These soldiers had volunteered to save others from being taken by force from their homeworld. They had sacrificed their futures so that others could live, secure to raise the next generation.

The man nodded at her, and others followed suit. She had to clear the area so Darak could come out, in his disguise. But these men deserved her thanks, as well. And perhaps she could give them a tiny bit of hope.

Not really sure why she did so, Jana lowered the scarf that covered her face so the soldiers nearest to her could see the glint of the crystal shards in the skin of her face. When the old soldier's eyes widened, she knew the Plectarans, at least, would have something to talk about tonight.

"Change is coming. Be ready for it when opportunity arrives. We may not get out of this unscathed, but if I can survive this..." she touched the largest crystal on her face that was embedded just below her eye, close to her temple, "...then perhaps our homeworlds can survive even more."

Jana pulled the scarf up, making sure it hid her permanent jewelry before she left the gathered soldiers. She beat a hasty retreat, dropping the tray exactly where she had taken it from. With any luck, Darak would storm out a few minutes after her, leaving by the front entrance, as they had agreed. She would shadow him for a few blocks, until he was able to find a discreet place to dump his disguise.

Then, all they had to do was find Seta. Jana had already re-tagged Darak. They would re-tag Seta, and everyone could translocate back to the *Circe*.

But Jana already knew she was going to stay behind. She had unfinished business with Kol, and this seemed to be the best opportunity she was going to get to see him dead. She would not leave the surface willingly, until Kol had been dealt with.

* * *

Jana rejoined Darak about fifteen minutes later. The plan had worked like a charm and much to her surprise, Seta showed up all on her own. She joined them in an alley off the main street of the bustling town.

Darak gathered her into a quick hug, his expression one of relief before he let her go and held her at arm's length. Seta was wearing more clothes than Jana had ever seen her in, but she was still underdressed for socially strict Mithrak.

"What happened to you?" Darak asked, noting the torn sleeve and smudges of dirt on Seta's pretty face.

"I ran into a bit of trouble and had to fight my way out since I couldn't use my Talent," she admitted. "I'll be okay."

"How did you find us?" Jana asked.

"I saw Jana come out of the hotel and followed her to the detention center. I waited outside, and when I saw her come out, I followed again," Seta explained.

Jana came forward and touched the tag to the bare skin of Seta's arm. "You should go back to the ship," she advised the other woman softly. "You both should." Jana included Darak in her admonition.

"But I want to help," Seta protested, although Jana had seen the way the other woman was trying to hard not to limp. She was hurt. She needed medical attention.

"Jana's right," Darak said in a firm voice. "You need to go back. Jana and I will stay here and finish the job."

"You should go too, Captain," Jana said, deliberately using his rank to put space between them. "You've already been arrested once. The Wizard I knocked out will sleep for a while, but eventually, he'll awaken, and they'll be looking for you."

Darak stepped closer to her. "I'm not going anywhere without you, Jana. We stand or fall here together."

She gauged his expression and saw that iron will that had gained him the position of StarLord at such a comparatively young age. He would not be dissuaded.

"So, I guess we'd better stand, then," she muttered.

Seta was convinced to translocate back up to the *Circe* with only a bit more prodding. She took instructions and a sitrep from Darak back with her. Jana sent the pre-arranged signal of a set sequence of clicks, which would hopefully go unnoticed by the Wizards' fleet, and a few seconds later, Seta was gone. Back up to the ship.

"We need to get off the street," Darak said, peering out from the dark alley near the end of town.

"We need to get out of town." Jana took the premise one step further. "There's little more we can learn from this group. Kol isn't here and likely won't be coming here. He sent that little worm Geranth to do the job in this town."

"So, we need to find out where Kol is," Darak stated the problem. "How do we do that?"

"I think I know how," Jana admitted. "I've been experimenting with the crystals. I think I can open myself up a little more. It might at least give us a direction."

Darak frowned. "We can discuss that later. Right now, how do we get from place to place on this planet? I don't see much transport tech. Is there such a thing as a speeder rental?"

Jana shook her head. "No. Mithrak has always been a tech-limited world by design of the founders. It was started as a religious colony. That's why our moral code is so strict and we have very little technology. We were ripe for the picking when the collective decided to annex us." She tried to keep the bitterness from her tone, but knew she failed. "There are no speeder rentals or high-speed transports. But we can get a couple of horses."

CHAPTER ELEVEN

"I know this place," Jana said a few hours later when they topped a rise and a new valley spread out before them. On the opposite side of the valley, a jagged tower stood out against the setting sun.

"Where are we?" Darak asked quietly. They hadn't spoken much since leaving the town behind on rented horses.

"If that's the tower ruin I think it is, we're in my home valley. My parents' farm spread out below the tower, and the herd grazed the land all around it. Jeri and I used to play there when we were little, even though it was forbidden."

"Why was it forbidden?" Darak wanted to know as they moved along at the horses' leisurely pace.

"The old folks said it had been a Wizard's tower, but I think now it was probably a school for training Talent, which on this planet has always been called Wizardry. When the collective came, using those same psychic powers but in much greater concentration, the people of Mithrak called them Wizards, too, and the name stuck. The tower was destroyed by the collective, and all its inhabitants were either killed or taken in the very first cull. Thousands were abducted from all over the planet, then, and each year, they come back and cull our people again, taking any new Talents that matured in the interim. The pattern has been repeating for almost a hundred years."

"Someday," Darak promised, "we'll put an end to the cull. We'll stop the collective, and prevent them—or anyone else—from enslaving Talents ever again. That's what the Council is meant to do. It was created so that Talents could be free to live as they choose without fear, and without abusing their power."

"It's a noble goal," Jana agreed. "But, having seen the power of the collective for myself, I'm not sure anyone can stop them. Even Jeri and Micah. With the control crystals amplifying the Voice and connecting all those Talents in real time, they are a formidable force. And that's not even counting their human army."

"We'll win the war one mind at the time if we have to," Darak said firmly. "We start with you, Jana. If you can be freed—even with the crystals still embedded in your skin— then others can be freed, too."

"Something strange happened in the detention center," she said, abruptly changing the subject. Darak let her because he sensed her discomfort with the previous topic.

"What happened?" he asked as the horses continued their leisurely gait down into the valley.

"One of the soldiers guarding the entrance to the cell block recognized me. He called me Star Killer and let me pass. On the way out, another of them stopped me and thanked me for saving Plectar. It looked like that group was made up of Plectaran warriors, and I think they must've been talking amongst themselves while I was in the cells with you. They had to know I was up to something, and they probably realized you weren't Geranth when you walked out of there."

"You think they let us go on purpose?" Darak was intrigued by the idea.

"I can see no other explanation. Plectarans seem to be a lot more loyal to their planet and their brethren than anyone realizes. I think they let me go because they're grateful to the Star Killer—even though I still don't remember how I managed to destroy a star." Her voice was filled with incredulity.

"Nobody knows how you did it, Jana. Ask Agnor when we get back. I think the Specitars have a whole team working on the problem. You did it, so they know it's possible, but how you did it remains a mystery." Darak had to smile, thinking about all those Specitars trying to puzzle out the actions of the beautiful woman who sat on her horse beside him.

To look at her, you wouldn't realize the core of steel in her being. But Darak was rapidly coming to understand that Jana was much more than a pretty face. She had an iron will and a brilliant mind. The more she remembered of her past, the more confident she became. It was like watching a flower blossom in the sun. She was reclaiming her life, little by little, and he felt privileged to watch it happen.

"I wonder if the Plectarans can be counted on?" Darak asked the question foremost in his mind.

Jana shook her head. "I wouldn't like to chance it. As it was, I was holding my breath the whole time we were near the detention center. All it would have taken was one loyal collective soldier to alert their platoon leader, and we would have been sunk. For that matter, if the platoon leader had been with his men, I don't think the Plectarans would have allowed me to pass. It was just luck that they were on their own and willing to look the other way for the sake of what I supposedly did for their planet."

"I think you might be underestimating their loyalty to you, Jana," Darak pointed out. "All those reports Zane passed along—at least the ones on the crystal he gave me—indicate that you did a lot more for their people than just that one mission. The reports show that you routinely sought ways to minimize losses among the soldiers. They respect that you for that. In fact, I think they love you, in their way, as a commanding officer who respected the value of their lives. I don't think that can be said of many other commanders under the control of the collective."

Jana was silent, but Darak saw the way her lips tightened.

The collective wasn't easy on its people. They were seen as pawns to be moved about the chessboard, and sacrifices were inevitable.

She was silent a while, and Darak realized they'd wandered into uncomfortable conversational territory again. Another change of topic was needed.

"If the tower was forbidden, would it make a good place to spend the night?" he asked. "I mean, we could always go back up to the ship, but I'd rather limit the number of transports, because they might be spotted and reveal the location of the *Circe*. It would be safer to stay down here. Besides, we should look after these horses and see if we can figure out our next move."

"The tower should be safe. Locals don't go there, and the Wizards have long since finished with it. But I already know my next move," she said, her voice going steely. "I'm going to rejoin my mind to the collective."

"What?" Darak felt panic and anger rise.

"On a limited basis," she assured him, turning to meet his gaze as their horses walked side by side. "I've already tested it a bit, and I believe that the crystals protect me, somehow. I didn't realize it until I started remembering things about Kol, but he has a tiny sliver of crystal in his palm. A little smaller than this one." She pointed to one of the tiniest bits of crystal on her face. "I think the masters might use it to keep their minds separate, yet part of the collective. I think it helps them remain in control of everyone else. At least, that what it seems to be doing."

"If that's true, then the blue crystals are even more important than we thought. We need to find out more about them," Darak said. "But I don't like you testing this yourself, in such a dangerous situation. Agnor would be the first to say that experiments need to be done under controlled circumstances where we can do all in our power to protect you. This..." He waved his hand around, indicating the entire situation, frustration in his every motion. "This is chaos. You could be captured. You could be sucked back under their power. You could die, Jana." His voice faded as emotion filled him. "I can't let that happen."

"And I can't let Kol live." The determination in her tone and adamant nature of her words shouldn't have surprised him.

Jana had led an armada of ships and thousands of soldiers in her time. The fact that she had been slowly recovering from traumatic injury had somewhat disguised the power of the woman beneath the shell of the injured girl she had been when Jeri last saw her. Darak knew Jana had been a strong woman in her own right, and it was good to see her finding her way again. But it was also inconvenient. Darak wanted to be in charge. He wanted to coddle her a bit longer. His every instinct told him to protect her.

He had to fight that instinct. He knew if he stifled her in any way, she would simply find a way around him. Possibly, she would leave him completely, and do what she wanted to do anyway. Jana had a strong will and Darak needed to respect that. He had to let her fly free and find her way back to herself, while still trying to watch over her. It would be a delicate balance.

"All right. We're agreed that Kol has to be stopped. Now, let's try to find a way to do that together." Jana looked at him, her jaw set at a stubborn angle. Darak had to give a little more ground to win her over. "If that means letting you contact the collective more closely, then let's do it under the safest circumstances we can arrange. Tonight, once we've made camp, we'll do this together. I'll monitor while you do your thing with the crystals. It's not perfect, but it'll have to do. Are we agreed?"

Jana seemed to consider his words, her head tilted to one side. Finally, she nodded. "All right. We'll try it your way."

They rode on until darkness fell completely. At one point, Jana sat up straight, pointing toward a farmhouse in the distance. She told him her family home had been around that spot before it burned, but there were lights on inside the new structure. Someone else had taken up residence, which negated any possibility of going there to see what was left.

In a way, Darak was glad. This journey back to her roots had to be hard enough on Jana as it was. Seeing the ground from which she had been kidnapped, and where her parents had been murdered, could be too traumatic. It was bad enough that they found themselves so close to her ancestral home and would be camping at a site that she and her sister had played in as girls.

He was no mind healer, but Darak thought he understood the power of memories. They could be amazingly good, or horrendously bad. He hoped he wasn't setting Jana up for heartache by camping in the ruins of the tower, but they had little choice if they wanted to stay on-planet.

The ruined tower was quite something, Darak thought as they approached the place sometime later. Much of it was still intact, though it was clear it had been ransacked and attempts had been made to tear it down. The front entrance, for example, was completely ruined, the gates torn off their hinges and large chunks of the outer wall ripped away.

Darak's expert eye also noted evidence of laser burns and sites on the outer structure where explosive rounds must have hit. It was a testament to the solidity of the massive stone structure that much of it had withstood the ravages of both the attack and time.

As they drew nearer, the tower loomed larger. It was actually quite massive and would probably best be described as a castle ruin, rather than simply a tower. There were remnants of outbuildings that had once been situated around the place and areas that might've been gardens where a stone fountain could still be seen.

"This place is amazing," Darak whispered, feeling the weight of the dark stone as night birds cried out softly above them.

They were able to ride the horses right through the massive stone arch, through the ruined gates and up into the ground level of the tower itself. Only once they were inside did Jana halt her beast and dismount. Darak followed suit. He had a portable lantern on his saddle, which he placed in the center of the room and switched to a higher illumination setting. The circular chamber was revealed in the soft glow, the walls scarred but still holding the remnants of ornate wall hangings and painted images.

"It looks just the same," she said quietly, taking a good long look around.

"It's in remarkably good shape," Darak observed. His legs weren't quite used to riding for hours, and he stretched as he looked around.

"The old timers said the Wizards tried to pull it down, but it wouldn't be budged. They claimed the magic of the place was stronger than the collective. I always liked that idea. Even more so now. I like the idea of anything that stood in defiance of the collective and survived to tell the tale." She turned around, looking at the roof of the circular main chamber. "It's kind of like me, in a way. Battered but not completely destroyed. Changed by the collective, but not shattered. And, like me, this building can be rebuilt someday. If we ever rid Mithrak of the collective and their culls."

Darak liked the way she was speaking. It all sounded much more positive than anything she'd said before. She was talking in terms of her own survival. It was a massive step in the right direction for her recovery.

"You've changed, Jana," he said honestly, looking at her as she refocused her gaze on him. She smiled, and he felt a lightness in his heart at the cautious radiance of it.

"I'm starting to remember myself," she admitted. "The files Zane gave me started a cascade of memory—some good, some bad. And being back here…" She looked around at the room again, then back to him. "Back on Mithrak, where it all started…" She dropped her hands and walked slowly toward him. "I feel like I've come full circle. I feel stronger. Not complete yet, but on my way there. I'm remembering who I was before the collective and who I came to be, even under their influence. And I'm deciding who I want to be in the future."

161

Darak stepped closer to her, putting his hands on her shoulders. "I'm happy for you, sweetheart." They shared a gentle smile. "I'm here if you need me, but you're making great progress. Even I can see that."

She stepped into his embrace, resting her head on his shoulder as his arms went around her. It was a hug of thanks, of comfort and of strength passing back and forth, multiplying as it reflected from one to the other. She was gaining confidence. He could feel it.

And he could see it in the things she had done. She'd broken him out of prison, for goodness sake.

"Did I thank you for rescuing me?" he whispered next to her ear, enjoying the moment of shared warmth.

"You rescued me first," she replied simply, touching him deeply. "It'll take a lot more than one little prison break to make us even."

He liked her wry humor.

They stood, enjoying each other's embrace for long minutes. Finally, Darak became aware of the noise outside. The wind had picked up. And the horses needed tending, though they hadn't wandered off, which was remarkable. He drew away from her by slow degrees, not wanting the moment to end, but knowing they had work to do before they could rest for the night.

"What shall we do with the horses?" he asked. "It sounds as if a storm has whipped up out there."

Jana stepped out of his arms and looked around again. "They can stay in here with us tonight. Jeri and I used to let our mounts drink from the old fountain, but we'll have to fill it from the well outside. Even though there are holes in the roof, the weather doesn't come inside. We spent many a rainy afternoon playing up here when we were children."

"Should we tie the horses to something?" Darak looked around again, looking for some sort of hitching post, or something they could use as one.

She smiled, walking up to the closest horse. "I'm not as good at this as Jeri is, but if I ask them nicely, I think they'll agree to stay in here where it's warm with us. We can build a fire in the old fireplace, too." She pointed to a massive fireplace along one wall. A stack of wood sat neatly next to it. "Nobody can see it from the valley, and the smoke goes out far above the tower, so it won't draw any attention. Jeri and I used that fireplace all the time when we were little, and nobody ever knew."

"There isn't much dust here," Darak observed, moving to lay a few logs into the fireplace.

"It never really got dusty here," Jana answered him while she went to the other horse and seemed to talk to it. "It's always been like that. The weather doesn't get in, and anything you put in here didn't deteriorate." She finished with the horse and spun around. "I wonder if the things we left are still here?"

Jana moved toward a far wall and pressed a series of latches. Within moments, a hidden closet opened and Darak could see the colorful fabrics within, even by the small light of their lantern. He was very conscious of their use of light and had positioned the lantern in such a way that nobody in the valley below would see the light up in the supposedly empty tower. They didn't want to draw any unwanted attention while they hid out up here.

Jana emptied the closet and brought the spoils over to Darak where he still crouched by the fireplace. He worked while she sorted through what he now saw was a series of mismatched sheets and pillows, towels and other small items.

"It's all odds and ends really, but Jeri and I managed to take some of the cast offs and bring them up here a piece at a time. We used to make a little tent out of the sheets and play make-believe games. This tower was our hideaway. We'd sneak up here when our parents thought we were doing chores. We would rush through our tasks and then come up here to play during our stolen hours. Some of the best memories of my childhood came from this tower."

Two small dolls fell out of a rolled up scrap of fabric, and Jana's breath caught. Darak lit the fire and turned to regard

Jana.

"Yours and Jeri's, I presume?" He pointed at the two rag dolls.

Jana's eyes sparkled with tears as she looked up at him. "Mama made those for us. They were our prized possessions." She lifted one of the dolls in trembling hands. "I'd forgotten we left them up here."

"You should take them with you when we leave. I think Jeri would like to have this little piece of your shared past, don't you?" He touched the hand-stitched face of the other doll.

"Oh, yes. We'll take them back with us," Jana said immediately. "If we live through this, I want Jeri to have this happy memory of our family. We both lost everything else when the Wizards came."

Jana touched the face of her doll with reverent fingers before rewrapping both dolls in the bundle they'd been in. She reached for the saddlebag she'd taken off her horse and placed the bundle, and as much of the scraps of fabric as she could fit, inside.

She cleared her throat before getting to her feet. "I'll see to the horses. There's a well out back, and I'll see if our bucket is still there."

"If it isn't, I can jury rig a sling of sorts from our supplies," Darak offered. She smiled gently at him and went to spend time on their big, four-legged companions.

He sensed she needed a little alone time to order her thoughts. It had to be difficult to come face to face with long-buried memories, but Jana was handling herself so well. It gave him hope that a complete emotional recovery wasn't as far away as he'd once thought.

* * *

Water fetched from the well in what looked like Jana's old bucket and horses tended for the night, Jana rejoined Darak by the fire sometime later. He had put the time to good use, unrolling their sleep sacks and spreading them before the fire. He'd also heated some of the food they'd brought with them. The hostelry where they'd gotten the horses had provided long-lasting travel rations, as well as some fresh food, for their journey.

"Smells good," she commented, placing her bucket—full of crisp, clean water—down next to the hearth.

Darak dished up the prepared food and handed Jana her portion. She sat cross-legged on the unrolled sleep sacks facing him. He joined her, and a few moments later, they were both eating a meal that tasted even more delicious because they were both quite hungry after their long journey that day.

They ate in companionable silence for a while before Darak offered up a possible topic of conversation.

"There's something different about this building," he said, not unkindly. "If we were on a higher-tech world, I'd say there was some kind of force field protecting everything within here, but I don't see any tech that would account for it."

"It's always been like this," Jana offered, eating her dinner. "We could leave sandwiches up here for a week, and they wouldn't go moldy. There's some kind of energy up here..." She trailed off, looking around the circular chamber. "But it's not evil. It's protective, whatever it is."

"There are certain spots on Geneth Mar said to be like this. Most of them have temples of one kind or another built nearby. Perhaps this planet is similar?" Darak mused. "If the collective ever lost power here, I know quite a few Specitars who would gladly make researching this place their life's work."

"Agnor?" she asked with a raised eyebrow.

"Oh, perhaps, but I think Ag is more suited to adventure than he realizes. He may think he's strictly a scientist, but I've seen him in battle, and I know there's more to him than meets the eye. He could be the *Circe's* next captain, if anything happens to me."

Jana didn't respond, and he realized he'd taken the conversation into depressing areas.

"Sorry." He tried to fix what he'd done. "I just meant that he's got the makings of a spy and a leader of men. He just doesn't realize it."

She left him hanging for a minute or two, but the she seemed to shake off whatever negative thoughts his careless words had brought up. She shrugged and the look in her eyes was far away.

"A lot of things make us find qualities within ourselves that we didn't realize were there. I never dreamed of commanding a starship, much less an armada, when I was a girl playing in this tower with my sister." She looked up at the domed roof high above them. "I was just starting to think about boys when the Wizards came. I thought maybe I'd find a nice lad and settle down in a few years. Start a family. Maybe start a herd with my father's help. That was as high as I dared dream. But then, I guess I showed some sort of aptitude, and the collective decided to turn me into a soldier and then a starship captain. And then, apparently, a Star Killer."

"I still can't believe that was you," Darak admitted. "I mean, I know you can do anything you set your mind to, but I'm flabbergasted by the idea that you were the one to pull off something that has puzzled all of our Specitars since it happened." Darak grinned at her. "You're going to be in great demand when we get back to Geneth Mar. Every Specitar with an interest in astrophysics is going to be knocking on your door to find out how you did it."

"If I remember, I'll tell them, but certain parts of my memory are still gone." She gave him a soft smile. "When we get back to the ship, I'll have to read the rest of those files Zane gave me. Each one I read brought back a little more of my past, but I couldn't go through them too quickly. There was too much. It felt like overload as each new memory came rushing back."

"We can do it a little at a time," Darak assured her. "And

I'm here for you if you need help. Any time, Jana. I mean that."

She looked at him, smiling softly. "Thank you." The moment drew out. "I mean that. I haven't always been the easiest person to be around during my recovery, and you've always been patient with me. If I haven't said thank you before, let me do it now."

"There's no need to thank me," Darak said, moving closer. "I would do anything for you."

CHAPTER TWELVE

Darak's words sounded so serious. She wasn't sure how to take them, but a little part of her heart stood up at attention, wanting more. Slowly but surely, the irreverent StarLord had worn away her defenses. She was afraid she was very much in love with the rogue and feared it would end badly for her when he moved on to someone else.

But would he?

Those last words sounded like maybe she might have a shot at winning his heart. The thing was, she didn't know enough about Geneth Mar society and Darak, in particular, to know what to expect of a more permanent relationship with him. Would he still want to be with other women?

Jana had unbent her moral code a lot since awakening aboard the *Circe* free of the collective, but there were some things she would never compromise on. If she was going to be in a permanent relationship with anyone, she wanted it to be exclusive.

But, then, she thought of what Seta had told her. According to the voluptuous navigator, Darak hadn't been with any other women since Jana had been rescued. Jana wasn't sure how much to believe of that claim, but her fragile heart wanted to believe it was absolutely true and that the reason he hadn't sought pleasure elsewhere was because he was falling in love with her and wanted to be faithful only to her.

A girl could dream, couldn't she?

After all, Jana had had her youth stolen from her by the collective. She had never been through all the normal things a young woman would go through when discovering attraction for someone else. All those innocent adolescent experiences had been denied her. As a result, she didn't know what to make of Darak and his solemn words.

So, she said nothing as he moved closer still, taking her in his arms and placing a tender, powerful kiss on her lips. He deepened the kiss, and moments later, she found herself lying on her back, the soft fabric of the sleep sacks beneath her.

They made love by the firelight, Darak's gentle touches saying more than his words. Jana felt like she was the only woman in the universe to him in those moments when he joined their bodies and pushed her toward fulfillment.

Darak was her lover in every sense of the word as she finally gave up resisting and let her heart fly free. She gave up denial and embraced the fact that, even if he could never fully return her love, she had given her heart—if only for this short time—to Darak of Geneth Mar, rogue and StarLord, the kindest man she had ever known.

* * *

Jana woke deep in the night to the sound of the wind whipping around the ruined tower. They were safe and warm by the fire and within the protection of the tower, but the wildness of the wind called to something in her spirit. She remembered nights like this from when she was a little girl.

She remembered how her mother would hold her. And how her father would let her stay up late with him by the hearth while he told her stories of his youth or of fantastical beings and the ancient Wizards who had once lived up on this very hill. In this tower.

And now, she was here. And she was one of the Wizards.

And her lover was a Mage Master. And he actually seemed to care for her in a way she had dreamed of when she was a little girl. He might not be her husband. He might not ever have that kind of staying power or ability to commit to her, but her heart was brimming with love for him, and his power sparked off her own in delicious ways.

He made her feel good in so many ways. Accepted. Cherished. Cared for. Almost…loved in return.

But she wouldn't talk about feelings if he didn't bring it up. She didn't want to be so needy. She didn't want to put him on the spot. She was very much afraid that if she asked where she stood with him, his answer would crush her fragile heart.

She watched him sleep, loving the way his face relaxed into sleep. He looked almost boyish, but she knew him well enough to know that, although the boy still lived within the man, the man was deadly and strong. A good combination in a warrior such as he.

Jana made herself stop gawking at him and get up. She dressed in her outer robe and went to sit in the exact center of the domed room. The mosaic of the floor came to a point here, a focus, if you will. She thought it might be a good place to start her experiments with the crystals that never left her.

She planned to rejoin the collective tonight, so she would have her answer by morning. Either she'd be lost again—in which case, Darak would find her and try to get her out again—or she would know more about their next move. If they even had one.

She had to know where Kol was, and if he'd already left the planet. If so, there was no point, really, in staying on Mithrak. But, if he was still here, she needed to know where, so she could hunt him down like the dog he was.

Taking a moment to focus herself, Jana began the careful exploration of the blue crystals and how they might help her rejoin the collective on her terms…

What Jana discovered that windswept night shocked and amazed her. Not only could she join the collective, but she was operating on a whole new level with the aid of the crystals. She was no longer simply a cog in the wheel—a mind to be used and pillaged at will.

No, the crystals did something. They made her something different. Something above it all. A mind to rule the others and never be subjugated to the collective again.

She was gaining an appreciation for how it all worked. She saw the structure of the collective from above and knew there were just a few minds like hers, free to use the collective power for their own ends and direct it like the puppet masters she had always envisioned.

Further, she realized the crystals in her skin made her one of the masters now. She was in the collective, but the others didn't seem to recognize the power of her mind or her individual identity. They simply were aware of her and moved on, sensing the crystals that shielded her identity from them as their smaller crystals did their best to try to shield their identities from her.

Proximity had a lot to do with it, as well, she realized. The closer minds were more open to her while the other puppet masters who were farther away were better hidden.

She saw Kol's oily mind, right away. He was close. Closer than she would have guessed.

They could reach his camp by tomorrow afternoon if they left in the morning after breakfast. And then, she would have her revenge. And perhaps after that, she could get on with her life...if she was still alive.

Realizing she could disconnect from the collective at will, she let the connection go, sealing her mind away from them. Silencing the Voice.

She felt a moment's pride for being able to do that now. She had gained control and confidence over the voyage to get here, and when she stopped to think about it, she realized just how far she'd come.

She went back to the sleep sacks, which Darak had joined together so they could share them, and slid under the covers with him. Morning would come in a few hours, and she had a plan now.

Tomorrow, she was going to kill Kol.

When dawn came, Jana was awake first. Much as she would have liked to bask in Darak's embrace a few moments longer, she was also eager to be on their way. She had a task to complete before she could get on with her life, and today was the day.

She left the bed and dressed, noting Darak's sleepy movements behind her as she poked at the fire. They would need water, so she put on her cloak and wrapped her head in the warm scarf she had been wearing on this journey. The wind was still up, so she would need it.

Taking the old bucket with her, Jana went around the back of the tower to the old well.

Darak watched her go with fondness. Jana had come so far, so fast. He had seen her at her most fragile, and it made his heart feel good to see her find her footing at long last. She was regaining her confidence and, with it, her sense of self.

She had been a powerful woman, even while her mind had been subjugated by the collective. She had been a warrior. A woman to be reckoned with. A leader people looked up to, not because they feared her, but because—as the Plectarans' loyalty had proved—they respected her. Perhaps they even loved her.

She had been formidable, then, and Darak knew she could be again. He was beginning to see the signs, and it pleased him no end. He liked strong women, and he especially liked an underdog who had been beaten down, only to come back stronger than ever before.

He saw that in Jana, and it made him admire her all the more.

There was no question in his mind that he was developing strong feelings for her. Where those feelings might ultimately lead would depend entirely on her. She had been forced into things too many times for him to be willing to even hint at manipulating her for his own gain.

For he was coming to realize that his life would not be complete without her in it in some way. He didn't want to think too far ahead yet, because everything was so up in the air, but when he let himself consider the future, he couldn't picture his life without her in it.

He just had to cultivate the patience to let her come to terms with their relationship—if there was going to be one—on her own. He couldn't force her. He would never force her. Not for anything in the universe. She would come to him on her own, or he would let her go... No matter how badly it broke his heart.

He was working on breakfast at the fire when he sensed a presence behind him. Darak stood and whirled, but he wasn't quick enough. He froze—not of his own volition—but because he'd been hit but a swift, incredibly strong, telekinetic wave. The maker of the wave stood just inside the door to the circular chamber, a smug expression on his hated blue face.

Kol had found them.

And Darak was well and truly trapped. Much as he hated to admit it, Kol's telekinesis—backed up by the full power of the collective—had stopped Darak in his tracks. He was getting a firsthand lesson in what made the collective so damned formidable.

One on one, Darak thought he probably could've taken Kol. But, with the collective power of all those hijacked minds and Talents behind him, Kol was stronger than any single person. Maybe Micah and Jeri—two of the most powerful minds on Geneth Mar—could have stood their ground, but Darak wasn't certain.

He couldn't even reach out to Jana with his telepathy. Kol held Darak's Talent in check as easily as he held his body in mid-motion. Darak couldn't even speak. He was caught, with no visible recourse. And he couldn't warn Jana.

She walked in from the outside, her scarf still tight around her head, and stopped short as she took in the scene.

"Kol," she whispered, dropping the bucket she had taken

from the well. Water sloshed over the sides.

"Ah, my little Jana. I've missed you."

Kol's voice was oily smooth. Repulsive. Jana remembered it well. So much had come back to her about the past in the last few days. She had almost all of it now, and what she still didn't remember, she could piece together from the Plectaran reports when she got back to the *Circe*.

If she got back to the *Circe*.

Somehow, Kol must have sensed her intrusion into the collective and come here to pre-empt her. She wasn't as ready as she would've liked to have been, but perhaps, this was for the best. Kol had apparently come alone. She hadn't sensed anyone outside—and she had been checking.

The puppet master could have fooled her, but any minds he brought with him should have been detectable. Which meant, he was probably here on his own. Cut off from the collective, as was his usual style. Operating on his own, using all the power of the collective that was still at his disposal through the tiny shard of crystal in his palm, but not sharing his own mind with the other puppet masters who together were the Voice.

"How did you find me?" she whispered into the quiet of the chamber, buying time as she figured out how to play this out.

"I had your memories of this place from when you were a child," Kol said unexpectedly. "I knew if you ever came back to Mithrak, you would probably not be able to resist visiting this shrine to the lost ways of your people. This place draws our kind and always has. It is a natural place of power, which is why we could never destroy it completely—no matter how hard we tried. But we made it work to our advantage. We've had sensors on the gate since we claimed Mithrak for the collective. We knew about you and your sister long before we culled you. I watched you grow and wanted you for my own." He licked his disgusting dark blue lips as she remembered his many cruelties.

"I've tracked many others in this tower since you were taken. They come here, betray themselves by being drawn here, and I get their images sent directly to my files. I make note of them, and on my next trip through—if they are old enough—I take them for the collective," he went on. "So, when you got here last night and the sensor at the gate sent me your image, I had to come see for myself if it really was you. The scarf hid your pretty face, but I saw enough to make me believe my little Jana had finally come home."

His smile sickened her. But maybe there was a way to play this to her advantage?

"I'm not really your little Jana anymore, am I, Kol?" she asked in a purring sort of voice as she moved slowly toward him.

Kol's hand was still outstretched, the crystal sliver in his palm glinting as it focused the collective's power on Darak, keeping him immobile. Kol's eyes followed her movements, his expression one of greedy avarice as he watched her body move. She felt dirty just from the look he was giving her, but she had to brazen it out. Darak's life—her life—and a whole lot more was riding on the next few minutes.

She had to think. If Kol didn't realize she had been messing around with the crystals in her body and spying on him from inside the collective, then she might just have an ace in the hole. If he expected her to be the same as she'd been before, he had another think coming.

And, if he'd only seen her with the scarf covering her face, she had a little surprise for him…

"You're still as gorgeous as you ever were. A little thinner, perhaps, but that's an improvement," Kol had the audacity to say.

"I'm thin because I almost died, Kol," she reminded him. "Didn't you wonder what happened to me after the battle over Liata?"

He frowned. "You weren't disfigured, were you? Is that why you hide behind that scarf?" He actually looked as if he'd be repulsed if she revealed scars. The superficial bastard.

She moved closer, trying to position herself at the proper angle. When she struck, she would have to get it right the first time. There would be no do-overs.

"I *was* disfigured," she said in a small voice, pretending a meekness that didn't suit her true personality.

It wasn't sympathy she saw in his eyes, but disappointment. The sick bastard only cared about her as his plaything. He didn't care about *her,* at all.

"We can get you fixed," he said after a moment's consideration. "I'll find the best cosmetic surgeons in the collective and make you even prettier than you were before."

"Why?" She stopped. She was close enough and, if she had calculated correctly, at just the right position. "So you can rape me again?"

Kol's anger was quick to follow her words. "What I choose to do with you is none of your concern. I will get a child on you, and it will rule the collective one day."

So, that was his sick plan. She should have known. Kol always wanted power. He didn't care if it came at the expense of others.

She had no doubt he wanted his child to be the ruler of the collective. Not because he would love the child and wanted it to do well. No, this was all about Kol and what he wanted. He saw his child as a stepping stone to his own increase in power and influence.

The bastard.

So she lied, wanting to see him twist.

"I can't have children," she said in a flat voice. "I was too badly injured. They had to take some pieces out."

"That won't do at all," he was quick to say in an angry tone. At that point, she wasn't sure Kol was entirely sane. His eyes were wild.

"It's okay. I got other pieces in return." She was aiming to confuse him, and it seemed to be working. Confounding the power-hungry puppet master was easier than she had thought it would be.

"What are you talking about?" he demanded, clearly

agitated.

His focus had shifted from Darak to her. She had his undivided attention, though Darak was still held immobile. He wouldn't be released from Kol's amplified telekinesis unless something much more drastic happened to Kol.

And she was just the woman to make that happen.

"Did anyone tell you what exactly happened to me above Liata?" she asked instead of answering his question.

"The control crystal failed. It must have been flawed," he spat out.

"It didn't just fail, Kol," she informed him. "It blew up. In my face." She tore away the scarf and let the light filtering into the room from the holes in the ceiling sparkle off the many shards of crystal embedded around her right eye and down her cheek.

Kol gasped, his eyes growing wide with fear. Good. She wanted to see that look on his face for the few minutes he had left to live.

"I've been looking for a way to get these sparklies out of my skin, but they don't seem to want to go." She took off her riding gloves, one finger at a time, revealing the gems stuck into her right hand and holding them up to the light. "They're kind of pretty, but also a bit of a nuisance. Don't you think?"

"You can't take them out," Kol babbled. "Once implanted, the crystal will never come out. How did you survive having so much? It's easy to overload…" He trailed off as if realizing he was speaking secrets he should not be talking about.

"Is that why you only have that tiny sliver?" She taunted him while she systematically isolated him from the collective, first in small ways, and then enveloping him entirely within her shielding that allowed only what she wanted to pass in or out. At the moment, she let nothing out, though she still allowed Kol the illusion of receiving power from the collective so he wouldn't realize the noose was already around his neck until it was much, much too late.

"It's not tiny. It's the largest of anyone's except the grand master," he claimed, like a child boasting after he'd received an insult.

Jana hadn't realized there even *was* a grand master among the puppet masters of the collective, but it made sense. Someone had to be pulling all the strings to keep the others in line. Though, apparently Kol was one of the more important of the puppet masters.

"That's interesting," she said, nodding. "But what would he make of my new jewelry? I assure you, there are much larger chunks, but they're in places on my body that only my lover will ever see. And that's not you, Kol," she said pointedly. "You were my rapist. My lover is someone I fuck because I want to, not because I've been tied down and forced."

"You liked it," Kol argued. "You wanted me."

"Sorry, no." She shook her head and tried to be cool, even though she was shaking inside.

She wanted to kill this bastard with her bare hands, but she needed the information in his mind. He knew things about the collective that the Council needed to know if the collective was ever going to be stopped. And the more she saw of what she had once been forced to endure, the more she vowed to make it her life's work to stop the collective and free all those trapped minds and souls.

"You disgust me, Kol. You're an animal, despite all your efforts to pretend to be civilized."

He raised his hand to her, and she felt the tickle of his power, but it was no match for her. With the stones in her body, she could pull power from the collective, if she wanted to—but she was rapidly discovering there was another, much stronger source of power closer at hand.

The tower was a place of power, and that power was coming at her request, filling her to overflowing and allowing her to shape it to her will. Right now, her will was to freeze Kol with her telekinesis—which had never been her strongest Talent—as Kol had frozen Darak.

Kol gaped as he discovered he couldn't move. Jana smiled.

The next thing was to free Darak. A simple snip of Kol's telekinetic line that had led to Darak, and he was free. She noted Darak moving behind her, but her focus had to stay on Kol, for now. She was enjoying this, but she wouldn't be cruel. She would get whatever information she could from the man before she decided his fate.

Before she'd wanted him dead, but now that she knew she could control him, she was beginning to think about taking him prisoner and bringing him back to Geneth Mar. Surely, there were people there who could discover all his secrets and use them against the collective much more effectively than she could do alone.

But, while she had him in her power, she wanted to get as much information as possible. Depending on what happened next, she might not get another crack at him. The planet was still crawling with the collective's troops and Talents. Any number of things could go wrong. She had to do what she could to learn more while she still had the clear advantage.

Kol seemed to know a lot about the crystals. She needed to know more, since they were apparently going to be a permanent part of her.

"Tell me about my pretty jewelry, Kol," she said in a deceptively idle tone as she lifted her hand to the light, watching the crystal sparkle. "Do you think it's going to kill me in the end?

Kol seemed entranced by the dance of light off her crystals, following the pinpoints of light with his black eyes.

"I don't know how you managed to survive so much," he breathed. Jana hid her smile. "Even the grandmaster only has a single gem. It's larger than all of ours combined, but it's still just one. You've got...how many?"

"There are too many slivers to make an accurate count," Jana replied, wanting to keep him talking. "But I know there are at least four or five that would equal ten karats or more."

"Ten!" Kol exclaimed. "The grand master's is only one karat. Mine is two-tenths, but only because I claimed it myself, in the mines. The others only get a tenth or less."

"How many others, Kol?" she asked calmly. "How many puppet masters rule the collective?"

His face shuttered, as if he suddenly realized he was talking about things he shouldn't mention. She could compel him to talk—she could even invade his mind and take all his memories—but she didn't want to sink to his level.

"Where are the mines?" Darak asked. Released from Kol's hold, he now stood behind the blue man. It looked like ready Darak was ready to jump Kol if he made the slightest move toward Jana.

But Kol wasn't going anywhere. She had him in her hold, and she wasn't letting go for anything.

Not surprisingly, Kol refused to answer Darak's question. Jana knew this information was critical. The crystal was what gave the puppet masters of the collective power. Without it, they could never control so many minds.

"Is that where you used to go on all those secret trips?" Jana asked. "Are you the mine master? Is that the job your brothers left to you? Digging in the dirt for rocks while they live in palaces of gold?"

"It's not like that," Kol's pride seemed to force him to say. "The mine master is the most trusted position."

Jana laughed. "Is that what they told you?" She took off her cloak, revealing a few more of the gems in her arm and going down her neck. The rest were hidden by the various layers of her clothing.

She watched Kol's reaction to her crystals. He was staring, and the sight of the larger crystals seemed to entrance him. Perhaps enough to be tricked into revealing vital information? She would have to test her theory and find out.

"I think they are using you, Kol. They make you find the crystals that they use to control everyone else. If you showed a little initiative, you could choke off the supply and keep it all for yourself. You could be grand master, Kol. If you control the crystal, you control the collective."

His eyes bulged as the thoughts ran through his mind. Something was going on in there, and she was very much afraid she was going to have to enter his mind to find out the truth. She didn't want to go in there, but she feared it would end up being the only way to get the information they needed in time.

Kol would be missed sooner rather than later. He'd come here alone, she was certain, but his guards were nearby and would look for him when he didn't return. They didn't have all day to do this.

"I am lord of the crystal planet!" Kol suddenly cried out, his body going rigid.

Jana and Darak both moved forward. Kol was having a fit of some kind, moving violently, even against Jana's telekinetic hold.

"He might be programmed," Darak said as he met Jana's gaze. "That grand master of his probably inserted a pain command if Kol started thinking too independently."

Jana frowned. She'd never heard of such a thing, but knew it probably was feasible given the crystals and the way they focused power.

"What should we do?" she asked Darak, Kol's shuddering body in the yards between them.

"If there's a failsafe, go in fast and take whatever you can get," he advised.

"I don't know if I can. I don't want to go into his mind."

"You're the only one who can, Jana. His crystal blocks all my probes," Darak admitted. "We need what he knows."

CHAPTER THIRTEEN

Jana realized the truth of Darak's words. The crystals weren't just for focusing power; they also made the user nearly impervious to outside attack, which is why she'd carried one as leader of the armada. Certain trusted leaders within the collective were given the scepters when they were on important missions. Each of the scepters was tightly controlled because of the power it represented—both the power to rule other minds and to be safe from psy attack while wielding it.

She focused again on Kol as his pain seemed to subside. She had to work fast, and she had to ask the right questions. She knew what Darak had meant by *failsafe*. If Kol could be programmed to feel pain at independent thought about taking over the collective from the grand master, then other commands could have been implanted—much more fatal commands. If she triggered one of those, she'd have to harvest what was left of Kol's mind before he died.

Grim. But necessary.

She had no love lost for Kol. Up until a few minutes ago, she thought for sure she was going to kill him herself, with her bare hands if necessary. But she had come to realize he was more valuable as a prisoner—if he survived the programming the shadowy grand master seemed to have put in place.

Kol would probably die, anyway, but at least she wouldn't bear the sole responsibility for it. The grand master had killed him as soon as he put those commands into Kol's mind. Jana would be the one to trigger them, so she did bear some responsibility, but she could live with that if it meant they could free others from the collective and possibly stop its advance.

She had to be cautious with her questions, but she also had to get the information. She thought carefully about what she would ask.

"Where is the crystal planet?" she asked finally.

"None of your business." Kol frowned and looked to be in pain again, this time, not as bad as before.

"Who works in the mines?" she asked, trying a different tack.

"Nobody," Kol spit out.

"Bots?" she mused. "I've never heard of any mining operation that didn't have at least a few organic minds running things, even if the heavy lifting was done by bots. So, tell me, Kol, who does the collective trust enough to have work in their crystal mines?"

"Me," he boasted, clearly triggering a pain response. "Just me!"

"Try again." She looked at him with disdain, and he bristled.

"You can't do this to me! I am your master!"

"Gee, uh... Let me check." She looked at the ceiling, rolled her eyes a bit and then looked back at Kol. "Nope. I have no master. Not anymore. And, yes, it does appear I *can* do this to you." She tightened her hold so that he couldn't move a muscle, letting him know in no uncertain terms that she was the master now.

Then, she relaxed it a bit, allowing him to speak and make small movements. Her control was fine, and she knew from prior experience that Kol himself didn't have that kind of finesse. His eyes widened as he realized her power.

"This isn't right," he protested, clearly still clinging to his delusions surrounding his own strength.

But Jana had had enough.

"I'll tell you what isn't right, you bastard. Subjugating people and stealing their power isn't right. Kidnapping little girls and raping them isn't right." She advanced on him with each sentence, anger in every fiber of her being, tears falling down her face, unheeded. "Separating me from my sister wasn't right. And killing my parents wasn't right." She stopped a few feet in front of Kol, his body paralyzed by the force of her will. "They never did anything to you! Nobody on Mithrak ever deserved what you did to us. Have done to us. For years! You stole our planet, like you steal our people and our free will. You steal our Talent and use it for your own selfish ends. *That's* not right." She paused in her tirade, breathing hard.

She saw the fear in his eyes, but she had to keep on pushing. "Now tell me where the crystal mines are or I'll crush you where you stand. You know I have the power. You'll never rule me again. You'll be lucky if I let you live."

Kol seemed to fear her. Good. She read panic in his eyes, and then, a sort of resignation came over his features.

"I can give you the mines. I am their caretaker," he said, pain entering his eyes again.

"Where are they? What planet?" she insisted.

She needed to know. Control over the crystal meant control over the collective. If she could stop more of the crystal from falling into the masters' hands, she could stop them in their tracks. And then—only then—would her life have been worth something.

She saw stopping the collective as her chance at redemption. And this blue insect wasn't going to stand in her way. She needed what he knew.

Kol blinked a few times. His mouth opened...

"Ip—" he whispered, breaking off as a spasm struck him hard.

And then, his eyes rolled back in his head as he sagged in

her telekinetic hold.

"Failsafe!" Darak yelled, coming up behind Kol, putting his hands on Kol's temples.

Jana knew what Darak was trying to do. He was trying to get into Kol's mind before he died. He was trying to salvage what information he could before the deadly command that must have been triggered by Kol's decision to speak of the crystal planet took full effect.

Harnessing all her the new power given her by the crystals in her skin and all the skill she could muster, she ripped into Kol's dying mind, taking everything and leaving nothing behind. She took the good memories with the bad. She would sort through them later.

She saw Darak in there with her, his mind as strong as hers, but the power not augmented by her crystals. She saw he'd saved a lot of data in an area that looked as if it had burned on the mental plane. That must've been the epicenter of the explosion. That was where the data they most needed would probably be hidden. If anything was left.

They had to work fast. As Kol's body died—and there was nothing they could do to save him now—his mind was shutting down, the memories fading as the organic computer that held them died. She literally saw his energy leaving his body, his thoughts going off somewhere she could not follow.

She had to grab what she could before it was all lost. Desperately, she sought for the information she most wanted—the location of the crystal planet.

There...

Almost...

And then, Kol was gone. She had saved what she could, and there was no more left. Kol was dead. His memories gone with him into another realm.

She let go of Kol's body and let it slip to the floor. Darak stood facing her, his expression intense.

"Ipson," he whispered. "That's the name of the planet. Did you get the coordinates?"

"I think so," she replied, a little shell shocked from what had just happened.

Her emotions were all over the place. She had gone from anger to anxiety to rage to furious mental activity as she pushed her skills to new heights and did things she had never contemplated doing before.

But they'd had to be done. And she had been the only one with the entrée into Kol's crystal-enhanced mind able to do it. Though...Darak had been there.

"How did you get into his mind?" she asked, still in a state of confusion and heightened awareness after such an expenditure of power.

"Look at his hand," Darak said, pointing to where Kol's right hand was stretched out on the floor.

In the center, where the sliver of crystal had been, was a black mark. The crystal had burned up, burning out Kol's mind with it.

"So that was the failsafe?" she asked.

"The crystals must be programmable. I think the crystal held the data that was shared with the grand master," Darak theorized. "It blew, but we were still able to get into his memories. I saw some of it."

"I got more. I just collected everything I could before his mind fled into the ether. I shoved it...somewhere..." She thought about it, not really understanding what she'd done in her moment of panic and need. "It's in this crystal," she said, holding out her right hand, rubbing the largest of the chunks that could be seen on her hand with her left forefinger. "I didn't realize what I was doing at the time, but I put his memories here. You're right, Darak. They function like data crystals but with way more capacity and different abilities..."

"We're going to have to study this in greater detail, but right now, I think we need to get the hell out of here. Kol came alone, but it probably won't be long before someone comes looking for him." Darak moved to the fire to gather up their belongings and douse the flames.

Prodded into motion by Darak's bustling around the fire,

Jana collected the water she'd brought in and dropped by the door, giving it to the horses, who had spent the night on the other side of the wide, round room. They had been calm throughout, though she knew from their swiveling ears and alert eyes that they'd been watching what had happened.

Jeri was better with horses than she was, but Jana petted their noses, taking a moment to unsaddle them. She left the saddles on the floor, knowing they'd be turning the horses loose when they translocated back up to the ship. There was no reason to stay. Kol was dead, and they now had vital information that had to get back to the Council.

She thanked the horses and told them to seek the farm in the valley below, hoping that whoever now lived in her old house would treat the horses kindly. She also made sure to erase any evidence of her and Darak's presence from the tack she was leaving behind in the tower.

When she finished, she turned back toward the center of the room where the confrontation with Kol had taken place. If they left his body there, would it not deteriorate, like the other things they had left in the tower over the years?

"What should we do with him?" Jana asked. "Do we just leave him here?"

Darak came to her as she stood over Kol's body. They both looked down on the shell that was left behind of the man who had caused so much misery.

"I think we should take him back to Liata and let them decide. He is one of theirs, even if he turned his back on his people in favor of power," Darak said unexpectedly. "Liatans have very strict beliefs about burial and the afterlife. We wouldn't want to do the wrong thing with one of their people."

Jana saw the sense in that. It wasn't about Kol, per se, but about Liata and keeping alliances strong. Much as she'd hated Kol, she wouldn't deny the Liatans their right to decide what happened to his body.

"I'll get them to send a stasis pod down from the ship," Darak said, trying to use his communicator. After a couple of tries with no response, he shook his head. "There's something strange about this tower. None of my tech gear works properly in here."

"But did you notice how your psi powers are amplified here?" she asked softly. "I bet you could 'path Agnor from here with no problem."

Darak was silent a moment, his gaze considering. Then, his eyes lost focus as he tried the telepathic message to his ship in orbit. A smile spread over his lips as he blinked back to focus a few moments later.

"Worked like a charm," he reported. "You're right about this place. It sounded like Ag was right next door, not on the other side of the planet. He's going to transfer a stasis pod on his next revolution in about fifteen minutes. I told him to aim for the area between the gate and the doorway, so stay clear of it until the pod arrives."

"Just enough time to finish cleaning up here and packing our things," she said, moving to do just that.

But Darak intercepted her. He took her into his arms, and she went gladly, clinging to him in the aftermath of the most distressing thing to happen since being stolen away from her home. She'd come full circle, at last. It had all started here, on Mithrak, in the valley not far below. It was sort of poetic that it ended here, too.

"There's time for this, too," he whispered, his mouth next to her ear. "Time to be grateful that we both made it through this alive. Time to begin healing."

"Thank you, Darak. You've been—" Her voice cracked with emotion as she clung to him, her head nestled on his shoulder. His warmth heated the cold places in her soul.

"Ssh," he crooned. "It is I who should be thanking you. You saved us both here today. You and your incredible power. I'm in awe of you, Jana." He rocked her from side to side, and something in her heart felt the first faint hint of joy as the realization slowly hit her that they were both still standing and Kol was actually dead.

She still couldn't quite believe it.

"It wasn't really me. It's the crystal," she began modestly, but Darak pulled away, smiling that devilish smile at her.

"Don't sell yourself short, sweetheart. It's you. And it's the crystal. But the crystal would be nothing without your beautiful mind to guide it. You overpowered Kol's hold on me, and for that, I owe you my life." He winked at her, and she felt a moment of happiness, even though they were still in danger every moment they stayed on Mithrak. "But we can discuss how I'll pay you back later. Right now, we need to get out of here, right?"

Darak let her go, holding onto her arms until he was sure Jana was stable. He watched her closely for any signs of instability. He could tell she was still somewhat in shock, but time was of the essence. They had to get away from Mithrak and report what they now knew back to the Council. The information they now possessed was too important to take chances.

He watched her as she finished packing. He helped, erasing any sign of their camp as best he could. They didn't have a whole lot of gear, so it was reasonably simple to break camp.

Before he knew it, they were ready, and the fifteen minutes were up. He went to the arched doorway and looked out. Sure enough, the pod, on its hoversled, was waiting. Darak jogged out to get it and brought it back into the chamber.

He saw the look on Jana's face as he bent to deal with Kol's lifeless body. She looked a little green around the gills now that they were out of the heat of combat. He paused.

"Why don't you let me handle this, sweetheart? Go outside for a bit and get some fresh air. Take the horses out and turn them loose, okay?"

She looked like she wanted to protest, but then relented. "If you're sure, I'll just take care of the horses."

He was glad she'd taken his offer of an out. He knew now that Jana was too sensitive a soul to deal with the taking of a life—even one as evil as Kol's—lightly.

Darak readied the pod and did a quick but thorough search of Kol's pockets. He knew the body would undergo microscopic examination when they got back to Liata. Spores and microbes in his body might tell them a lot about his travels.

Kol had been too highly placed in the collective to let pass uninvestigated. If the Liatans didn't want to do it, Darak would exercise his right as a StarLord and bring the body to Geneth Mar. In fact, he might just do that first, anyway. Oh, he'd return Kol to his home planet, eventually, but not after they'd gleaned every last bit of information his body might betray.

Some information might come a little easier though, Darak discovered, as he palmed a small handcomp and sets of miniature data crystals Kol had hidden in the inner hem of his jacket. Had the man been foolish enough to bring all his data with him on a mission he'd tackled all alone?

Apparently so. Though a closer examination would be needed of the handcomp and crystals. Agnor could start on that aboard the *Circe*, once they got back up there. Jana could help, since she was probably the most likely of them to know collective access codes and systems. It would give them something to do on the trip back home—which they'd be making at top speed. No saving the engines with this kind of booty on board.

Darak couldn't help the sense of satisfaction that threatened to overtake him. But the mission wasn't finished. They weren't home free yet. They weren't even out of danger yet.

He had to stop counting his accolades before they were due. He had to get everyone home in one piece first and the data delivered before he could count this mission the success it looked like it was going to be.

Still, he couldn't help a feeling of grim satisfaction as he hoisted Kol's limp body into the pod and shut the lid. With a flicker of satisfaction, he turned on the stasis field that would preserve the body until it was delivered to the Specitars back on Geneth Mar. After they were done, he would see that Kol made it back to Liata—if the Liatans wanted to claim him.

He suspected he'd have to spend a little time in diplomatic talks with the leaders of Liata to discover exactly what they wanted done with Kol. He'd made an assumption about them wanting him back, but Darak needed firmer information than his best guess.

Darak sighed. He was learning firsthand something his cousin Micah had said many times... A StarLord's work was never finished.

Jana was glad to escape the tower chamber. She didn't want to think just yet about what had happened inside, but she felt a sort of burgeoning sense of freedom, deep in her soul. It was an uncomfortable feeling, to be sure, because it had come at the expense of another's life.

She had hated Kol, and thought she wanted him dead, but the way he'd died... It left a very bad taste in her mouth. He had been killed, ultimately, by his master.

Even her tormentor—a puppet master himself—had answered to a crueler master. Even Kol had been a slave to the collective in the end.

Poetic, in a way, but still very distasteful.

Jana tried her best to shake off the feeling as she rubbed her hands over the horses. They'd been good companions on their short journey, and she wanted them to know she appreciated their hard work on her behalf. Jana believed she was able to get her message across with gentle touches and kind murmurs, in addition to the mental nudges she was able to deliver.

In fact, she was better at the mental contact than she'd ever been as a child. That thought gave her some satisfaction. Not all the skills she'd gained as an adult were deadly, apparently. That gave her a sad sort of hope for the future.

Maybe...just maybe...she could stop the killing. Maybe Kol would be the last life she took. Maybe since he had started it all, he would be the end of it, too.

A girl could hope.

Movement to her left caught her eye, and Jana turned her head to see a soldier step out of hiding near the ruined gate. His hands were up in the air in the universal sign of peace, but he was a collective soldier. A big man. Plectaran, maybe.

If he realized Kol was inside…and dead… Well, it wouldn't be good. Jana started sending out feelers. Where was one soldier, there usually were others.

Sure enough, she detected eight other minds nearby, arrayed in a wide spread around the yard. Except for the door to the tower chamber behind her, she was surrounded. Dammit.

"Are you the Star Killer?" the first soldier—the only one who had so far revealed himself—asked in a quiet voice, shocking her.

She'd expected a friendly ruse, or maybe an outright confrontation about Kol if they'd traced him this far. Instead, she got what seemed to be the standard Plectaran greeting where she was concerned.

"I am Jana Olafsdotter," she replied in a tired voice as she rested her hands on the back of one of the horses. "I recently learned that you Plectarans call me Jana Star Killer, but I have to admit, at this moment, I have no memory of the event."

The soldier came forward, his steps unusually hesitant for a Plectaran who outsized her two or three times. He also knew that his platoon-mates had her surrounded, so there was no reason for him to be so unsure. Jana frowned, resting her forehead against the horse's flank for a short moment.

If they were caught, then so be it. She'd taken Kol's life— not necessarily intentionally—but the result was the same regardless of her shifting intentions. Kol was dead, and she'd been part of the cause. If his soldiers wanted to exact revenge for it, then she was almost resigned to it.

Frankly, she didn't know where her life would go now. She'd had her revenge, and she was at loose ends. She didn't have a purpose any longer—except maybe the larger one of trying to help end the collective's hold on all those innocent worlds, once and for all.

But that plan was nebulous, at best. Sure, she had some valuable information now, taken from Kol's dying mind, but that didn't seem real.

Or, at least, not as real as the nine soldiers who all had her in their sights. A full platoon, minus the Talented leader who would be joined to the collective, she realized. Now that was interesting. Their babysitter was absent. Was that by their purposeful design? Or was it merely a coincidence?

"Word has spread among the Plectarans of your presence here on Mithrak," the soldier went on. "I am Rilet. You won't remember me, but I was part of one of your strike teams back when you were a battalion commander. I'm glad to see you whole and well, Commander."

The man's smile was wholly unexpected. Jana straightened and looked up into the soldier's violet eyes. He was a younger one, and very striking.

"I am no longer a commander, Mr. Rilet. Please call me Jana," she said tiredly. It had been one hell of a day, and it wasn't even noon yet. "I'm glad you've survived life in the collective, regardless of whether or not I remember you. To be truthful, much of my time in the collective is a blank to me. I don't remember most of the people I once knew and served with. I am sorry."

"Do not be sorry, Lady. We Plectarans remember for you, as was prophesied." An older man stepped forward from out of the greenery on the western side of the gate and came forward. He knelt on one knee when he was about three feet from her, much to her surprise.

Rilet knelt, too. And, one by one, the rest of the platoon came out of hiding and joined them, kneeling before her. Jana wasn't sure what to do.

They were all looking up at her with various expressions of awe on their faces, and it made her distinctly uncomfortable. Then, she recalled the older soldier's words.

"There's a prophecy about me?"

"Aye," said the old soldier, standing and facing her with his hands held respectfully clasped in front of him in a show of peace. "You, who were the savior of our entire solar system. You, who survived the crystal shards." Jana's hand went reflexively to the crystals in her face. All the men followed her actions. "You are the Star Killer. The savior of Plectar and of all the worlds swallowed whole by the collective."

"You've got to be kidding," Jana objected, just on principle.

The old soldier smiled and shook his head. "It is already done, Lady. The wheels of fortune have been set in motion, and you are already playing your part, though you may not realize it. We, of Plectar, will aid you on your way. The information you carry is vital to the fulfillment of the prophecy, and we are pledged to do all in our power to help it come to pass."

Darak picked that moment to step through the doorway of the tower chamber. Jana was relieved to see he had left the pod behind. No doubt he'd sensed what was going on and took the precaution of leaving Kol in his pod, hidden inside.

She really should've 'pathed him, but she didn't know what to say. This situation was way too strange to be able to explain quickly.

"Hello, friends," Darak said in a jovial voice. "Can we help you?"

The old soldier smiled and shook his head at Darak. "You have already helped us, StarLord. Now, I think, it is time for you and your lady to be on your way."

"Are you part of Kol's protective detail?" Jana asked, knowing she couldn't let these men leave—which amazingly, they seemed prepared to do—without warning them.

"We are, and we've already taken precautions. We'll take no blame for what transpired today, though our leader will. It is no loss. Our current platoon leader is one who truly enjoys his work, in the worst possible way. He volunteered to join his mind to the collective and has been licking Kol's boots as he climbs the ladder. He is Kol's protégée in all things." The old soldier grimaced. "He will not be missed."

"Then, you know what happened?" Jana had to ask.

The old soldier nodded solemnly. "It was foretold."

The rest of the platoon got to their feet and headed toward the gate at the old man's nod. He lingered to talk with her a moment more.

"We will not soon forget this day, Lady. We honor your sacrifice and your courage. You will always have a place on Plectar, if you wish it."

Jana was taken aback. Plectar was famous for its warriors—and for its history of being off limits to casual visitors and immigrants. It was a mostly closed society that didn't really welcome outsiders. For her to be invited there was a very big deal, indeed.

"I am honored," she said with all due gravity. "Please, tell me, Sergeant, what is your name?" She had read his rank from his insignia, but his name was nowhere on his uniform. Collective soldiers were numbers and ranks, not individuals.

"I am Balthazar of the White Rock Clan," he said, bowing his head slightly, though he didn't break eye contact. "Rilet is my nephew. Every member of our platoon is from White Rock, and we are all honored to have been the ones to whom fell the task of helping fulfill the prophecy. It brings great honor to ourselves and our Clan."

"Please tell me you truly won't pay for this?" Jana asked worriedly. "We can find room for you, if you need safe passage away from here." She looked at Darak, and he nodded.

"There's no need for you to die today, men," Darak said in a strong voice, backing her up. "We'll take you with us."

But Balthazar held up one hand, palm outward. "Your offer does you great credit, StarLord, and will not be forgotten, but we are safe. All has been foretold. But you two need to get out of here, soon, if you're going to carry out the rest of your part of the prophecy. Do not delay. We will guard the entrance, but we cannot stay for much longer. Ten minutes is all I can promise you, Lady."

"It will be enough," Jana said, making a snap decision. She stepped forward to take Balthazar's hand when he would have turned to leave. She looked up into his blue-violet eyes and felt the power of his hand in hers as she offered him a handshake—the sign of respect among soldiers. "Thank you, Balthazar of the White Rock Clan. I may not remember everything from my past, but I will never forget you."

Daring greatly, she reached up and kissed the old soldier on the cheek. His grin lit up his face as he let go of her hand and turned to rejoin his men. Jana and Darak had found an unexpected ally in the Plectarans. Now, it was up to them to use the next ten minutes wisely and get as far away from Mithrak as fast as the *Circe* could take them.

Darak ran back inside and returned with the stasis pod on its sled, then hit the communicator. Jana sent the horses off with a slap to each of their rumps, and her good thoughts in their minds. They cleared the courtyard about thirty seconds before Agnor locked on to her, Darak, and Kol's stasis pod.

The next thing she knew, she was on board the *Circe*, and Agnor was already breaking orbit. Darak went straight to his captain's chair while Kol's pod had been transferred directly to a storage hold. Jana was a bit dazed by all that had happened, but she got her bearings quickly and took her usual seat at the console off to one side.

It would take some time for her to process everything that had gone on down on the surface of Mithrak, but it looked like they had made a clean getaway. She only hoped Balthazar's prophecy was correct, and he and his men would be safe from repercussions when it was discovered that Kol was nowhere to be found.

She assumed the other puppet masters might eventually send troops to investigate his disappearance from the collective. But then again, they were probably used to Kol being absent for extended periods. For one thing, from all he'd said and what she'd learned from his mind in those last moments, he was the only one besides the grand master who knew the location of Ipson, the crystal planet.

He dropped out of the collective routinely, when he did his runs to Ipson to pick up loads of crystal or oversee the operations there. He also liked to drop out of the collective when he wanted to play his twisted sexual games—like the ones he'd perpetrated on her. She was disgusted to realize that she hadn't been his only victim; though, for a while there, she was apparently his favorite.

Jana did her best to put aside the disturbing thoughts as the *Circe* was put through her paces, racing at top speed back toward Council space. For Jana, they couldn't reach Geneth Mar soon enough. She wanted to get rid of Kol's information and pass it along to those who wouldn't feel so soiled by going through his data.

Having been brutalized by Kol, Jana took no pleasure in examining his thoughts or data. She just wanted to forget it all and move on with her life.

She knew she would have to talk to the mind healer again when she got back, but she was ready. She was ready to move forward and discover whatever would come next on her journey.

CHAPTER FOURTEEN

The *Circe's* top-of-the-line engines were straining, but it didn't take too long to get away from Mithrak and back into Council space. Darak stayed on the bridge throughout, knowing that the information they'd obtained was too important to not give their escape his full attention.

As soon as Agnor was free, Darak asked him to send a priority message via telepathy—untraceable and impossible to intercept—to Darak's uncle, Vizier Brandon. Darak took a few minutes to compose the message he wanted to Agnor to send and then sent it to Ag's console. Darak saw Agnor read it, then sit up straight as if he'd received an electrical shock. Agnor then turned wide eyes on Darak, a million questions in his astute gaze as he looked from Darak to Jana and back again. Darak only nodded.

"Send the message, Ag," Darak 'pathed privately to his friend and first officer. *"I don't want to talk about it yet in front of Jana. She's been through a hell of a lot, and I don't want to add any pressure just now. I'll tell you what I can as we fill in Uncle Brandon."*

What followed was a solid hour of Agnor acting as telepathic go-between for Darak with his uncle back on Geneth Mar.

Darak told his uncle everything he'd learned about Ipson and the structure of the collective, but knew he didn't know half the story. Jana would have to be debriefed in detail, but he would put that off until they returned to Geneth Mar. She would need time to come to terms with everything that happened, and Darak would do all in his power to give it to her.

Toward the end of his conversation with Vizier Brandon through Agnor, Jana seemed to sit up and finally take notice of things on the bridge. She sent Agnor a suspicious look, probably noting his glazed-over eyes, which indicated a deep 'path.

Jana turned her astute gaze on Darak, and he caught his breath at her beauty once again. She was still wearing the ragged clothing of Mithrak, and smudge of dirt graced her left cheek, but she had never been lovelier to him.

She sent him a message through his console, apparently wanting to keep her questions private.

Is Agnor 'pathing the Council? she asked via a text message. He simply looked at her and nodded. She turned back to her console and spent a moment composing a new message, then sent it to him. It contained a set of coordinates.

He sent back a one-word query. *Ipson?*

This time, Jana nodded.

Darak wasted no time in sending the coordinates to Agnor's console so he could append them to his next message. The location of Ipson was all-important. If something happened to prevent them from reaching Geneth Mar, at least they would have this vital piece of intel.

Darak didn't breathe easy until he had Agnor's acknowledgment that the coordinates of the crystal planet had been sent and received with the utmost seriousness by Darak's uncle. Agnor also passed along the message that Brandon was arranging for a priority-docking slot for the Circe and immediate debriefs for her crew—especially those who had been down on the planet.

The others would be questioned, too. In fact, Agnor had taken his time stealthed in orbit to record numerous observations about the way the collective used their ships.

He'd also taken detailed notes on ship design, capabilities and anything he had seen them do. Being so close to a planetary operation by the collective was something that had never been done before. The *Circe's* refitted stealth system had made it all possible, and Agnor had taken full advantage to learn whatever he could about the way the collective operated in space.

Those who'd been on the ground could tell the Council more about the personnel, and Jana had a great deal of intel stored on just one of her blue crystals. They would have to figure out a way to transfer that without causing her harm, but first, he insisted on her being allowed to speak with the mind healer, if she wanted.

Darak made sure to get Brandon's assurances of that provision before he let Agnor end the conversation. Although Agnor's expanded abilities allowed him to 'path across stay systems, it was also rather taxing on his personal energy. By the time everything had been settled, Agnor was slumping in his seat, his normally rigid posture suffering the effects of his mental fatigue.

"Are you all right, Ag?" Darak asked aloud, breaking the intense silence of the bridge.

"Just a little tired. I'll be fine in a few minutes," Agnor assured his captain and friend.

Jana surprised him by getting up and going over to Agnor. The bemused Specitar watched her walk toward him with a look of weary concern on his face.

And then, Jana touched Agnor's forehead with her right index finger, and the crystals along her arm glowed softly. It looked, though he could hardly believe it, that the power of those crystals was flowing through Jana, down her arm to her fingertip, and into Agnor.

She released him a moment later, and Agnor sat up straight, reinvigorated. Darak had never seen anything like it.

Jana turned and walked over to Darak, a slightly smug smile on her face.

"It seems…" she bent to whisper near his ear, "…that

there are other ways to amplify and restore power other than sharing sex."

He liked her playful mood and snagged her around the waist, pulling her down to sit on his lap. She went willingly, smiling at him as she put her arms around his neck. He dipped his head to kiss her.

"But it's not nearly as much fun," he whispered just before taking her mouth in a joyful, playful, wonderful kiss.

* * *

With Agnor reenergized, he was able to man the bridge while Darak and Jana finally took a few minutes to shower and change. They were still covered in the dust of Mithrak, and their clothing smelled of horse, which wasn't exactly appropriate attire for the bridge of a starship the caliber of the *Circe*.

But Darak wasn't one to stand on ceremony. He simply lifted Jana in his arms as he stood from his captain's chair and whisked her away to his cabin. As long as they were together, all would be well. He just had to keep believing that.

Thankfully, Jana didn't try to shut him out. She let him undress her in his cabin and didn't protest as he squeezed them both into the tiny shower stall. They bathed in the tight quarters, spending more time kissing and nibbling on interesting bits of each other's bodies than actually getting clean, but somehow, they managed.

Lying in bed with her after they had cleaned up and decided to take a short rest before rejoining the others, Darak traced the gems that wound their way up her arm and down the right side of her body. He loved the way she sparkled, but he had been concerned about the crystal's effect on Jana's mind and health for a long time. It seemed, finally, that she'd gained some mastery over the crystal that was now part of her, and he couldn't be more pleased.

"You've come a long way since the battle above Liata," he said softly, still tracing patterns on her skin.

"I've learned a lot in the past few days about who I was and what I am now," she answered in a contemplative tone. "I also know more about who I want to be. But there are more blanks in my past that I need to fill in before I know for certain what the future may hold."

"Then, you don't believe everything is predestined like your Plectaran friends?" He smiled as he dipped his head to kiss his way slowly down her right arm.

"I don't know what to believe about all that, honestly, but it was handy that they believed it, at the time. We could've been in a whole lot of trouble if they hadn't let us go."

Darak stilled, meeting her gaze. "They wouldn't have been able to stop us, Jana. You know that. But it would have gotten messy."

Nodding slowly, she finally agreed. "I guess I have to get used to the power these crystals have given me. I was what I believe must have been a mid-level Talent before Liata. Now…I don't know what I am. I don't think Kol could even comprehend the amount of crystal in my body. And he only saw my hand and my face. What about all the rest?" She gestured down her right side where some of the largest of the chunks had lodged.

"Does that worry you?" Darak asked in all seriousness.

"A little," she replied. "But, if it was going to kill me, I think it would have already done so. For whatever reason, my mind and body have reached some kind of balance with the crystal, and it seems content to stay where it is, for now."

"You speak of it almost as if it were alive," he observed.

Jana tilted her head, considering. "Maybe it is, in a way. It's certainly nothing like any other crystal I've ever encountered, though I'm no mineralogist. But it works a bit like a data crystal, only with way more capacity. And it meshes with my mind and amplifies my Talent. It feels as if it's accepted me. In the early days, it felt like it was weighing me and waiting to see if I was worthy or something. As I remembered my past and learned about what I had done through the Plectaran reports, it seemed to finally accept me more fully. And then, it started to open up to me and show me things..."

"What sort of things?" Darak prompted when she didn't continue right away.

"I can't really put it into words, but it was like the crystal revealed how it all worked to my inner mind when I needed it. Like it had consciously decided to cooperate with me or something." She looked down, shaking her head. "Or maybe I'm just imagining it all, and they're nothing but chunks of sparkly rock." A small laugh accompanied her words, but Darak knew there was some significance to her ideas.

"It's not for me to judge, but I think you might want to discuss some of this with Agnor. He has the most scientific mind I know, and I'm certain he's fascinated by the crystal. He's talked about it with me many times, positing theories on how your scepter might have worked before it blew up in your hands. I think he'd be willing to listen to anything you had to say on the topic. As would many of the other Speicitars when we get back home." He leaned in to kiss the tip of her nose. "You're going to be a very popular girl when we get back to Geneth Mar."

Jana groaned. "Do I have to?"

Her whining complaint was comical, but also truthful. She didn't really want to be the center of all kinds of fuss again. Jana wanted a quiet life from now on, but she suspected she might not get it.

Darak hugged her, kissing her neck. "I'll be with you through it all, I promise."

Jana's breath caught. That sounded serious. Almost like a declaration...

She met his gaze and knew it was time to ask the things she'd been afraid to ask.

"Do you mean that, Dar?" she whispered.

He grew solemn. He must've felt the weight of her words and was responding in kind.

"I do." He took one of her hands in his. "I can't really

imagine my future without you in it, Jana."

She thought maybe she stopped breathing for a moment at his declaration. Could he mean...?

"I feel the same way," she whispered.

To her surprise, he slid out of the bed to kneel at its side, but kept hold of her hand.

"Then, will you join your life to mine, forsaking all others? Will you marry me, Jana, and make me whole?"

She blinked, and the tears in her eyes rolled down her cheeks, unheeded. She saw raw emotion in Darak's dark eyes as he squeezed her hand.

She slid out of bed to land beside him on the carpeted deck, facing him, still holding his hand. There was just one more thing she needed to know.

"Do you..." She hesitated. The answer to her question was all-important. "Do you love me?" she whispered.

"Oh, Jana..."

Her heart sank, fearing she'd put him on the spot and his answer wasn't going to be what she wanted to hear. He dipped his head closer, kissing her cheek as she waited and worried about what he might say next.

"Jana, I never knew what love was before I met you."

Her heart lifted. Their eyes met and held as he went on.

"You have opened my heart and nurtured my soul in ways nobody ever has. I want to be with you for the rest of my days, Jana. You, and only you, in case you had any doubts." The devilish glint in his eyes returned, warming her from within. "I love you with all my heart. And that's something I've never said to any other woman. You are my everything. The other half of my soul. Please say you'll be mine forevermore."

"I didn't think..." she began, but she saw the way his hopeful expression grew concerned. She realized he had the same doubts that had been in her mind only moments before, and she rushed to reassure him. "Oh, Darak, I love you, too. And, if you really want to marry me, it would be my honor to join my life to yours. I don't think I could survive without you by my side and propping me up. Your strength is my savior, and your love is a gift I never expected to receive."

She was crying happy tears when he pulled her against him, hugging her close as they both knelt on the floor at the side of the bed, repeating their words of love over and over between kisses.

There would be much to do once they got back to Geneth Mar, including endless questions about the collective and their new understanding of it. The crystal planet would have to be investigated, and the crystals themselves would have to be studied much more closely.

But that was all secondary, as far as Jana was concerned. Her top priority was now spending time with the man she loved. She had a lot of living to make up for, and she wanted to do it all with Darak.

She once again had a family. Her sister was alive and well, and they could see each other any time they wanted. She had a new brother-in-law in Micah, who was also Darak's cousin. But, most of all, she would be going back to Geneth Mar an engaged woman with a wedding to plan—and a life full of love and happiness to look forward to.

As far as Jana was concerned, she and Darak had both earned a little time off to enjoy being together. Sure, she'd do her part and tell anyone who wanted to know about how the collective worked and what her crystals could do. She would do what she could to help end the collective, so that other trapped souls might find freedom, but she was through with traveling for now.

At least for a little while.

She wanted to get married. She wanted to do all those girly things she had dreamed of when she was a child. And she wanted to bask in the love she thought she might never find.

Then, maybe, she'd be ready to go another round against the collective. After all, her crystals seemed to be a pretty good weapon against the Wizards, and she owed them for stealing so many years of her life.

Yeah, she would teach the grand master and all the puppet

masters that payback was a bitch.

And her name was Jana Star Killer.

EPILOGUE

Agnor did his best to learn all he could about the collective and the crystals on the voyage back to Geneth Mar. For one thing, Vizier Brandon kept 'pathing him with questions—especially as they drew closer to the planet. For another, Agnor was simply fascinated by everything Jana and Darak had uncovered while down on Mithrak, put together with the things he had observed from orbit.

He'd already put together several reports for the Specitar community that he would publish when he reached home. For now, to preserve security, he was only speaking via direct telepathy with Vizier Brandon. No regular comms were originating from the ship, and they were running silent all the way back home. Their cargo was too precious to risk.

* * *

They made it home safely and, as Agnor had expected, Darak and Jana were immediately whisked away for private debriefings with the Viziers. Agnor went to the Specitar's Council, to answer to his own colleagues. He published his findings for private dissemination among the Specitars and was first debriefed then invited back many times on successive days to expand on his observations and answer a multitude of questions.

Everyone, it seemed, wanted to examine Jana's crystals, but she was in seclusion, protected by the Shas who were her family. Agnor was able to procure one or two slivers of the crystal that Darak had managed to save after his initial treatment of her injuries. He'd taken small slivers out of her skin before they'd healed over, but any further removal had proven both imprudent and impossible.

The Specitars were thrilled with the tiny specs of crystal they had to test, regardless. Teams of specialists were organized, and Agnor was asked to consult with each one on an ongoing basis. He was something of a celebrity among his colleagues for having been aboard the *Circe* and observing all of these things firsthand. Not many of the scientifically-minded Specitars had the courage or desire to serve aboard a ship—especially not one with as dangerous a reputation as the *Circe*.

Which is part of the reason, Agnor was told later, he had been promoted to the exalted rank of StarLord. There were precious few StarLords, and none of those currently active were Specitars. Which made Agnor a rarity among rarities.

In addition, the Specitar Council had decided there was no one better qualified to serve as captain to their newest science and exploration vessel, the *Calypso*. It was an immense honor, and one Agnor could not turn down, no matter how much he would miss his shipmates on the *Circe*.

Especially now, when they were so close to discovering all the secrets of the blue crystal. Agnor knew exactly where he would take the *Calypso* first. He was headed, with all possible speed and stealth, to Ipson.

# # #

ABOUT THE AUTHOR

Bianca D'Arc has run a laboratory, climbed the corporate ladder in the shark-infested streets of lower Manhattan, studied and taught martial arts, and earned the right to put a whole bunch of letters after her name, but she's always enjoyed writing more than any of her other pursuits. She grew up and still lives on Long Island, where she keeps busy with an extensive garden, several aquariums full of very demanding fish, and writing her favorite genres of paranormal, fantasy and sci-fi romance.

Bianca loves to hear from readers and can be reached through Twitter (@BiancaDArc), Facebook (BiancaDArcAuthor) or through the various links on her website.

WELCOME TO THE D'ARC SIDE…
WWW.BIANCADARC.COM

OTHER BOOKS BY BIANCA D'ARC

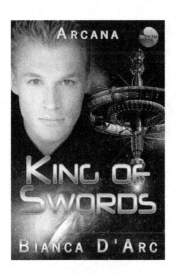

ARCANA
KING OF SWORDS

David is a newly retired special ops soldier, looking to find his way in an unfamiliar civilian world. His first step is to visit an old friend, the owner of a bar called *The Rabbit Hole* on a distant space station. While there, he meets an intriguing woman who holds the keys to his future.

Adele has a special ability, handed down through her family. Adele can sometimes see the future. She doesn't know exactly why she's been drawn to the space station where her aunt deals cards in a bar that caters to station workers and ex-military. She only knows that she needs to be there. When she meets David, sparks of desire fly between them and she begins to suspect that he is part of the reason she traveled halfway across the galaxy.

Pirates gas the inhabitants of the station while Adele and David are safe inside a transport tube and it's up to them to repel the invaders. Passion flares while they wait for the right moment to overcome the alien threat and retake the station. But what good can one retired soldier and a civilian do against a ship full of alien pirates?

RESONANCE MATES 1
HARA'S LEGACY

It's a serious game of cowboys and aliens when three psychically gifted brothers try to protect the one fragile, empathic woman who holds all their hearts against a menacing alien threat.

Montana rancher Caleb O'Hara's precognitive abilities saved his family from an alien attack that annihilated almost everyone on Earth. Now the aliens have come to study the remnants of humanity. Caleb knows the only way to ensure the safety of his young wife, Janie, and his beloved brothers, Justin and Mick, is to keep the family together on their isolated ranch.

All three O'Hara brothers love Jane. They grew up next door to the young, empathic beauty and she stole all their hearts at one time or another, though she married Caleb. Caleb foresees the shocking truth of what they have to do in order to survive, and Caleb's visions never lie.

They'll have to come to terms with a new world, and an evolving relationship, all while finding a way to protect two newborn babies who are innocent pawns in the aliens' deadly game. Somehow, this one talented family holds the key for humanity's survival on this new, conquered world called Earth.

TALES OF THE WERE ~ THE OTHERS
ROCKY

On the run from her husband's killers, there is only one man who can help her now… her Rock.

Maggie is on the run from those who killed her husband nine months ago. She knows the only one who can help her is Rocco, a grizzly shifter she knew in her youth. She arrives on his doorstep in labor with twins. Magical, shapeshifting, bear cub twins destined to lead the next generation of werecreatures in North America.

Rocky is devastated by the news of his Clan brother's death, but he cannot deny the attraction that has never waned for the small human woman who stole his heart a long time ago. Rocky absented himself from her life when she chose to marry his childhood friend, but the years haven't changed the way he feels for her.

And now there are two young lives to protect. Rocky will do everything in his power to end the threat to the small family and claim them for himself. He knows he is the perfect Alpha to teach the cubs as they grow into their power… if their mother will let him love her as he has always longed to do.

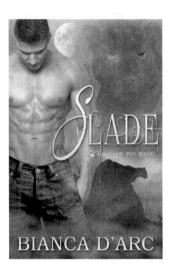

TALES OF THE WERE ~ THE OTHERS
SLADE

The fate of all shifters rests on his broad shoulders, but all he can think of is her.

Slade is a warrior and spy sent to Nevada to track a brutal murderer before the existence of all shifters is revealed to a world not ready to know.

Kate is a priestess serving the large community of shifters that have gathered around the Redstone cougars. When their matriarch is murdered and the scene polluted by dark magic, she knows she must help the enigmatic man sent to track the killer.

Together, Slade and Kate find not one but two evil mages that they alone can neutralize. Slade finds it hard to keep his hands off his sexy new partner, the cougars are out for blood, and the killers have an even more sinister plan in mind.

Can Kate somehow keep her hands to herself when the most attractive man she's ever met makes her want to throw caution to the wind? And can Slade do his job and save the situation when he's finally found a woman who can make him purr?

Warning: Contains a tiny bit of sexy ménage action with two smokin' hot men..

TALES OF THE WERE ~ REDSTONE CLAN 1
GRIF

Griffon Redstone is the eldest of five brothers and the leader of one of the most influential shifter Clans in North America. He seeks solace in the mountains, away from the horrific events of the past months, for both himself and his young sister. The deaths of their older sister and mother have hit them both very hard.

Lindsey Tate is human, but very aware of the werewolf Pack that lives near her grandfather's old cabin. She's come to right a wrong her grandfather committed against the Pack and salvage what's left of her family's honor—if the wolves will let her. Mostly, they seem intent on running her out of town on a rail.

But the golden haired stranger, Grif, comes to her rescue more than once. He stands up for her against the wolf Pack and then helps her fix the old generator at the cabin. When she performs a ceremony she expects will end in her death, the shifter deity has other ideas. Thrown together by fate, neither of them can deny their deep attraction, but will an old enemy tear them apart?

Warning: Frisky cats get up to all sorts of naughtiness, including a frenzy-induced multi-partner situation that might be a little intense for some readers.

TALES OF THE WERE ~ REDSTONE CLAN 2
RED

A water nymph and a werecougar meet in a bar fight… No joke.

Steve Redstone agrees to keep an eye on his friend's little sister while she's partying in Las Vegas. He's happy to do the favor for an old Army buddy. What he doesn't expect is the wild woman who heats his blood and attracts too much attention from Others in the area.

Steve ends up defending her honor, breaking his cover and seducing the woman all within hours of meeting her, but he's helpless to resist her. She is his mate and that startling fact is going to open up a whole can of worms with her, her brother and the rest of the Redstone Clan.

TALES OF THE WERE ~ REDSTONE CLAN 3
MAGNUS

A tortured vampire, a lonely shifter, and a deadly power struggle of supernatural proportions. Can their forbidden love prevail?

Magnus is the quiet brother. The one who keeps to himself. But he has good reason for his loner status. Two years ago, he met a woman. Not just any woman. This woman made his inner cougar stand up and roar. Even in human form, he purred when she stroked him, a sure sign that she was his mate. And mating is a very serious thing among shifters. Too bad the lady had fangs...

Mag discovers Miranda being held captive. She's been tortured to the point of -madness. Mag frees her and takes her to his home, nursing her back to health and defying all convention to keep her with him. He doesn't ever want to let her go again, but he knows the deck is stacked against them.

When a vampire uprising threatens, Mag and Miranda are in the middle. More than just their necks are on the line when a group of vampires seek to kill them and overthrow the current Master. But they have powerful allies, and their renewed relationship has made both of them stronger than either would ever be alone.

Can they stay together forever? Or will the daylight—and their two very different worlds—tear them apart again?

WWW.BIANCADARC.COM

CPSIA information can be obtained at www.ICGtesting.com
Printed in the USA
LVOW04s1834020915

452548LV00018B/856/P